MY VERY END OF THE UNIVERSE

Advance Praise for

MY VERY END OF THE UNIVERSE

"*My Very End of the Universe* is indispensable reading for anyone who loves fiction that defies categorization—and for anyone who simply loves engrossing stories cast in superb prose. Each of these novellas-in-flash is exquisite in its own distinct way, and collectively they demonstrate what is possible when we break the traditional confines of form and dare to invent something new."

—LAURA VAN DEN BERG, AUTHOR OF *THE ISLE OF YOUTH*

"Mothers and daughters, fathers and sons, family dogs, all the dramas, distilled, through flash, more potent than ever. *My Very End of the Universe* offers five outstanding examples of the novella-in-flash form itself, along with indispensable essays from the authors on what this blending of short and long can do."

—JANE CIABATTARI, AUTHOR OF
STEALING THE FIRE AND *CALIFORNIA TALES*

"In tornado-flung trailer parks and icy lakes, citrus groves and drugstore aisles, the characters of *My Very End of the Universe* yearn to soar like Superman but are, more often, prayed for. Daughters struggle to rescue mothers, sons clobber the weak, outlaws menace and bedazzle—and in 1893, a newborn says 'Hello?' in a tiny, astonishing voice. Compact, intense, and thrilling, these five novellas-in-flash show us that even in the smallest spaces, we can learn how to fly."

—REBECCA MEACHAM, AUTHOR OF
LET'S DO AND *MORBID CURIOSITIES*

my very end
OF THE UNIVERSE

five **NOVELLAS-IN-FLASH**
and a study of the form

Tiff Holland   **Meg Pokrass**   **Aaron Teel**
Margaret Patton Chapman   **Chris Bower**

Rose Metal Press

2014

Rose Metal Press, Inc.
P.O. Box 1956
Brookline, MA 02446
rosemetalpress@gmail.com
www.rosemetalpress.com

Library of Congress Control Number: 2014949055
ISBN: 978-0-9887645-8-3

Cover and interior design by Emily Kent
Cover art: *Stardust*, by Echo Eggebrecht

This book is manufactured in the United States of America and printed on acid-free paper.

MIX
Paper from responsible sources
FSC
www.fsc.org   FSC® C011935

TABLE OF CONTENTS

INTRODUCTION

IN 2006, WHEN WE DECIDED that publishing books of hybrid work would be Rose Metal Press' mission, flash fiction was our first focus. Back then we called these stories "short shorts," a catch-all name encompassing the myriad monikers people used to refer to stories around and under 1,000 words, including "sudden fiction," "quick fiction," "fast fiction," and many more. Within a few years, the name "flash fiction" came to predominate, and seemingly simultaneously, the popularity of the form skyrocketed.

By 2010, we had noticed another genre growing in popularity among writers that was searching for a common name and definition. In various pitch letters and reviews, we heard it called the "flash fiction novel," the "novella-in-shorts," the "vignette novel," the "flash novella," the "novel-in-stories," the "linked short story collection," and eventually, the term that we decided to use, the "novella-in-flash." These works are novellas composed entirely of standalone flash fiction pieces organized into a full narrative arc. We have come to realize that this form has a history and tradition, but they have been obscured by its lack of a name. With this introduction to *My Very End of the Universe,* as well as with the book itself, we hope to help give a name and definition to this fascinating and versatile genre, drawing much-deserved wider attention to the form.

The name "flash" is particularly apt and illustrative for both of these genres: they surprise, they blaze, they make you blink. One way to describe the interplay of flash fiction and novellas-in-flash is to think of each flash as a star. Stars stand alone. They appear in the sky as singular sparks of light, each one possessed of its own flickering beauty. In nearly every era and culture, humans have named the stars and then taken those beloved luminous points and connected them in the sky into shapes and stories. Novellas-in-flash are like those constellations: writers linking their flashes together into a larger image— into narratives deep with possibilities.

Although literature is not commonly characterized as a durational art form, approaching it as such has its uses. For whatever else it is, literature—like music, theater, dance, and film—*is* a durational art form, achieving a particular effect on its audience based on the length of engagement. The novella and flash fiction forms are among the most duration-focused of genres, since their public images, for better and for worse, center upon their lengths.

In his 1842 *Graham's Magazine* review of Nathaniel Hawthorne's *Twice Told Tales,* Edgar Allan Poe wrote that "the fairest field for the exercise of the loftiest talent" outside the realm of rhyming poetry is "the short prose narrative," which he defined as "requiring from a half-hour to one or two hours in its perusal." According to Poe, longer forms such as the novel are "objectionable" because they cannot be read in a single sitting, and thus they deprive themselves and their readers "of the immense force derivable from totality." He goes on to point out that "Worldly interests intervening during the pauses of perusal modify, annul, or counteract, in a greater or less degree, the impressions of the book. But simple cessation in reading would, of itself, be sufficient to destroy the true unity."

Perhaps because of the title of the book he was reviewing, the term that Poe chose for this ideal short prose narrative during which "the author is enabled to carry out the fullness of his intention" was the "tale." But of course there are plenty of other names—the flash, the short story, and the novella among them—for texts that provide the reading experience praised by Poe during the duration of which "the soul of the reader is at the writer's control" and "there are no external or extrinsic influences—resulting from weariness or interruption."

In fairness, Poe warns, too, of the dangers of being too brief and of engaging the reader for such a short duration that, despite the intensity of the piece, no lasting impression is made.

The novella-in-flash takes the best of both of its namesakes' lengths, blending the extreme brevity of the flash with the longer—albeit still brief—arc of the novella. The strengths of this hybrid form are manifold and not purely durational, but one of its strongest and most appealing traits is certainly the way in which the novella-in-flash mixes the quick and the sustained into a single whole that may—if a reader wishes—be perused in one pass, but which coheres into a unity that will linger in the mind for a much greater time than the book took to consume.

To help define the novella-in-flash form, we'll need to talk not just about word count, but also about other crucial episodic and structural components of the genre. That being said, word count is not a bad place to start. The typical consensus on approximate form lengths is as follows:

Micro-Fiction: Up to 100 words
Flash Fiction: 100–1,000 words
Short Story: 1,000–7,500 words
Novella: 20,000–50,000 words
Novel: 50,000–150,000 words
Epics: Over 150,000 words

These categories vary slightly from source to source and also from genre to genre, depending on whether one is writing science fiction, say, versus literary fiction.

For the purposes of this book, the two categories of greatest interest are obviously those of flash (both fiction and nonfiction) and the novella. In the case of the former, each of the five novellas-in-flash included here adhere fairly rigorously, on a story-by-story basis, to the 1,000-words-or-less limit.

In the case of the latter, though, these novellas depart

considerably from the word count range of 20,000 to 50,000 words. The shortest of the bunch, Chris Bower's *The Family Dogs,* weighs in at under 5,000 words in its entirety. And even the longest, Margaret Patton Chapman's *Bell and Bargain,* tips the scales at just over 12,000 words. But word count alone is not what makes the individual stories in these collections flash, and word count alone is not what makes them cohere into novellas either.

When pressed to go beyond word counts to briefly outline the primary attributes and elements of the flash genre, writers and critics frequently—and usefully—reach for analogies. In her introduction to *The Rose Metal Press Field Guide to Writing Flash Fiction,* Tara L. Masih cites a description of rain from Stuart Dybek's story "Nighthawks," which says: "Each drop encases its own separate note, the way each drop engulfs its own blue pearl of light." Masih explains that, in this way, "a successful flash enchants us, each small story successfully rendered engulfing us for a brief moment [...] in its own brand of light, or truth. And the effects linger on, sometimes for decades."

Similarly, in his introduction to *The Rose Metal Press Field Guide to Writing Flash Nonfiction,* Dinty W. Moore offers a comparison from Judith Kitchen by way of identifying what—beyond word count—defines flash nonfiction: "I often use a snowball metaphor," she has said. "You've got all this stuff out there called snow but when you gather it all up and really pack it together, you know, and you throw it off, there's a sting. I think with these short pieces—even when they're quiet and meditative—the effect is a little sting." Flash is characterized by compression, immediacy, and tension, blending the concision of poetry with the narrative tools of fiction.

Unlike flash, novellas are not themselves a hybrid form. The traditional definition of a novella, per Merriam-Webster, is "a work of fiction intermediate in length and complexity between a short story and a novel." Aside from length, novellas are often characterized by their lack of subplots, as well as by their tendency to focus on individuals as opposed to a bigger and more sprawling social canvas.

But when the novella's traits of extended conflict and character development, accumulation and accretion to create a single, unified effect, and conclusions that often hover on the edge of major change are set in tandem with the aforementioned traits of flash, that's where hybridity enters and that intersection is where the novella-in-flash gets its distinctive form and power.

The novella-in-flash is valuable because it does something that other forms don't do, allowing the author to build a world that is compact but complex simultaneously. Often novellas-in-flash have a staccato feeling because of their numerous breaks: their plentiful starts and endings and the way that many of the individual stories stop short of where a chapter in a traditional novel or a longer short story would conclude. Other novellas-in-flash can have a dreamy effect, dropping the reader into situations they can't remember walking into and shifting them to new situations before they may feel done with the old ones.

It's not as easy to get buried or lost in the story the way a reader might in a novel that's thick and immersive, but the many gaps and separations and new-yet-continuing stories force the reader to pay closer attention—to not get lulled—while also creating a whole fictional reality as a longer novel or novella would do. There is also a great deal of room for structural play in the novella-in-flash: authors can span a very short period of time or a very long one, using the emptiness between stories to serve as bridges or moments or leaps. The requirement that each piece of the novella-in-flash must be a complete and standalone flash also lends itself well to non-linear time structures and the use of multiple narrators.

Over the years, various authors have written tales that either are or resemble novellas-in-flash, but they simply haven't been calling them that, partly because no agreed-upon name for the form existed and partly for marketing reasons. Novellas are famously difficult to sell, so many authors prefer not to call their books novellas or have them categorized as such, resolving instead to define them as novels. And as editors Masih and Moore have demonstrated, although both flash fiction and nonfiction have long histories extending back hundreds of years in many cultures, the term "flash" has only gained currency and prominence as the correct and agreed-upon name in the past two decades or so. Thus, many authors could not have said their novellas or novels were comprised of flash chapters even if they had wanted to.

Italy, England, and France all offer proof that this genre trend arose earlier than many readers might think. For instance, Giovanni Boccacio's 14th-century collection of novellas told in 100 stories, *The Decameron,* deploys flash techniques within its highly conceptual framework of brief narratives told by a set of seven young men and three young women who have fled the city of Florence to escape the ravages of the bubonic plague. Also created in the 1300s, Geoffrey Chaucer's *The Canterbury Tales* makes use of flash-esque strategies with its premise of a story-telling contest among a group of pilgrims making their way from the London district of Southwark to the holy shrine of Saint Thomas Becket at Canterbury Cathedral. Heavily inspired by *The Decameron,* Marguerite de Navarre's *The Heptameron* consists of 72 stories all bound by a frame narrative and dealing cohesively with themes of romantic love and lust.

More contemporarily, Joan Didion's 1970 book *Play It as It Lays,* with its brief and largely self-contained short chapters, operates as a kind of novel- or novella-in-flash *avant la letter,* as does Sandra Cisneros' 1984 coming-of-age book *The House on Mango Street* with its connected fragments and vignettes. You could also argue that the 117 numbered and titled vignettes in Evan S. Connell's 1959 book *Mrs. Bridge* are flashes, and thus that this book is a novel-in-flash. The 527 brief and jumpy segments that comprise Mary Robison's 2001 book *Why Did I Ever* not only serve to give body to her narrator's ADHD, but also operate as flash fictions that cohere across the tale's longer arc. And Sarah Shun-lien Bynum's 2004 book *Madeleine Is Sleeping* also functions as a novel-in-flash.

Over the past few years, more and more novels- and novellas-in-flash have been appearing. Some of them, as before, are not named as such, but a number of them have embraced the novella-in-flash moniker, including Matthew Salesses' 2013 book *I'm Not Saying, I'm Just Saying,* which consists of 115 titled chapters or flashes, as well as Matt Bell's 2012 abecedarian collection of flashes about fatherhood called *Cataclysm Baby* from the Mud Luscious Press Novel(La) Series. Rose Metal Press' own *Liliane's Balcony: A Novella of Fallingwater* (2013) by Kelcey Parker also operates as a novella-in-flash, using the form as a vehicle for multiple characters and points of view that constellate on one fateful day at the famous Frank Lloyd Wright home. *All the Day's Sad Stories* (2009) by Tina May Hall is also arguably a novella-in-flash, as is Aaron Burch's 2010 book *How to Predict the Weather.* One could also make the case that Sarah Manguso's 2008 fragmentary and lyrical illness memoir *The Two Kinds of Decay* is a memoir-in-flash.

Here at Rose Metal Press, we've been smitten with the novella-in-flash form for some time, beguiled by the concision of the individual pieces and the way they connect, breathe, and build into a larger narrative. They are a little bit like the finale at a fireworks show: each single shell explodes with precision and flare, searing the eye before fading; the booming whole of all the explosions combined leaves the audience gasping and satisfied.

We're now in our ninth year of running an annual chapbook contest for manuscripts of flash fiction or nonfiction. About five years ago, we started to see a trend as we read through the pile of submissions: more and more writers were repeating characters and settings, linking their flash pieces together to build a longer story. Our 2011 collection of five chapbooks chosen from the finalists of our 2009 and 2010 contests *They Could No Longer Contain Themselves* included two novellas-in-flash: Elizabeth J. Colen's *Dear Mother Monster, Dear Daughter Mistake* and Tim Jones-Yelvington's *Evan's House and the Other Boys Who Live There*. Both of these books push the boundaries of the form, using multiple narrators and large spans of time broken down into self-contained episodes.

That same year, our chapbook contest winner was the novella-in-flash *Betty Superman* by Tiff Holland, which quickly sold out and is reprinted in this book. Then the next year, 2012, the same thing happened: out of over 100 flash manuscripts, our guest judge Randall Brown chose Aaron Teel's *Shampoo Horns,* another novella-in-flash. We were experiencing a marked increase in fully connected or loosely connected narratives in our chapbook submissions, and our judges and readers were reacting enthusiastically to the form. *Shampoo Horns,* too, sold out within a year and is reprinted in this book.

We found much to admire in the form, and started to think more critically about what makes successful novellas-in-flash work, what compels writers to use the form, and why novellas-in-flash are such a delight to read. We began to conceptualize the book that would become *My Very End of the Universe* as a way to showcase exceptional examples of the form in practice, while also examining and defining the genre. We envisioned a book that was both a gripping, gratifying read and a tool for teaching and learning.

We started with the two winning chapbook reprints (Holland's *Betty Superman* and Teel's *Shampoo Horns*), and sought out three other authors working in the novella-in-flash form. Happily, in doing so, we acquired Chris Bower's *The Family Dogs,* Margaret Patton Chapman's *Bell and Bargain,* and Meg Pokrass' *Here, Where We Live.* We were thrilled with how the five manuscripts used the novella-in-flash form in different ways as befitted their characters, settings, and individual writing styles. Adding to the fun was that each novella-in-flash we've included explores complicated family relationships and the very ideas of home and family, but each book uses the genre to tackle these subjects in a different way, presenting further opportunities to study craft methods within the form. To augment this study and assist in the teaching of the genre, we asked the authors to write short process essays to accompany their novellas-in-flash.

Flash writers often are drawn to the novella-in-flash because it allows them to capitalize on the short form skills they've been honing for years while simultaneously experimenting with extended narratives. As you'll discover as you read the five books collected here, the novella-in-flash offers writers elasticity and creative license. As Tiff Holland points out in her essay, sometimes writers have a character too big for one single story that they want to reveal story by story rather than in a novel. Or sometimes, as Aaron Teel discusses, the writer is trying to use the form to replicate the swirling non-linear sensation of remembering a time or event. Chris Bower applies a different tactic in dealing with memory, delving into the significance of who gets to tell the story and how that affects what details get included. Meg Pokrass talks about the freedom that using standalone stories allows for ordering and reordering until the perfect arc presents itself. And Margaret Patton Chapman explores the importance of omission in the novella-in-flash—how the form allows much of the connective tissue to be left out, creating more room for the reader to make imaginative leaps with the writer.

While giving writers all manner of new ways to approach their characters, themes, and narrative structures, the novella-in-flash offers readers the detailed specificity of flash combined with the satisfaction of hanging out with the same characters for a while and seeing them change. When we were searching for a title for this collection, we considered a number of phrases alluding to elements of the novella-in-flash form, as well as words that centered on family narratives. In the end, we wanted something that captured the texture and impression of novellas-in-flash rather than elements of form or subject. "My very end of the universe," taken from a sentence in the title story of *Betty Superman*, seemed to sum up a magic particular to novellas-in-flash: the ability to focus intensely and specifically—a primary attribute of flash—on a character's world for a sustained period of time—a key element of a novella.

The short duration of the novella-in-flash does not allow for much extra context or commentary—there's not a whole lot of setting these characters against the backdrop of world events, for instance. But the novella-in-flash does allow for immediacy and intimacy: the reader is dropped into the character's life, into their very end of the universe, from the very first story.

That immediacy is combined with a need for engagement from the reader. The gaps or silences between each flash can heighten the reader's sense of participation and interactivity. In novels there is background and filler and context. In novellas-in-flash there is just each flash piece and the white space connecting it to the next story. But that emptiness is part of the beauty of a constellation: where some people see a bear, others see a dipper. Each culture has shaped the stars into likenesses that represent their myths and realities. The novella-in-flash leaves space for interpretation and imaginings from the reader, a refreshing opportunity in our sometimes overly expository literary culture.

We are excited to see how this genre grows and develops as more writers try it out and experiment with inevitable variations. We hope that this book will speed the novella-in-flash on its way into the common literary lexicon, while also delighting readers with characters and tales that map onto the mind's eye and stay awhile. Here in one book, readers will find the stars, the constellations, and the star chart—all the makings of a stellar journey.

—ABIGAIL BECKEL & KATHLEEN ROONEY
Rose Metal Press, 2014

MY VERY END OF THE UNIVERSE

1 | TIFF HOLLAND

Written in Stone:
How Subject Dictates Narrative Form

Betty Superman

WRITTEN IN STONE:
HOW SUBJECT DICTATES NARRATIVE FORM

> "Every block of stone has a statue inside it and it is the task of the sculptor to discover it."
>
> —MICHELANGELO

FLASH, LIKE POETRY, is an art of pure essence. That's what I love about it: the spark, the quick uptick, the unblurred moment. Flash was the only way to write *Betty Superman* because the character of Betty was so big. In a novel, she would have been like Godzilla—she would have trampled everything else. She required enough room to come fully into view, hence the use of the novella format, but she still needed to be tightly contained, hence the use of flash. The novella-in-flash was perfect for her.

Still, I didn't start out writing a novella or even a flash or series of flashes. The first piece I wrote was "Dragon Lady," and I wrote it as a narrative poem several years before I wrote any of the other pieces. I composed "Dragon Lady" as a character sketch. I thought I would write other poems that would then turn into a book, but I found instead that there was an entire, complete narrative line within the piece. It never fit anywhere else until I started to draft the flashes that would eventually be the rest of *Betty Superman*.

At the time, I fought writing prose. I only wrote poetry and was actually insulted when a famous poet told me I had "an instrument for fiction." However, his comment stuck with me and a few months later I started writing fiction, or, as my mother called them, "partly-trues."

I started writing poetry when I was eight years old. I wrote a few stories, mostly for creative writing classes, but I was in love with the idea of the "line." I memorized a lot of poetry. I played catcher on a local softball team throughout school and was advised to "chatter" to distract the batters. I recited poems, thoroughly throwing off the concentration of many would-be hitters. Some complained to the umpires!

My favorite poets when I first started writing were Robert Frost, Carl Sandburg, and even at an early age, Sylvia Plath. I loved narrative poetry first (and still) more than lyric poetry, which seemed to me, when I was young, like beautiful pictures, but without focus. I loved poems of characterization such as those found in Edgar Lee Masters' 1915 *Spoon River Anthology*, which I realize now definitely affected my evolution as a poet. That anthology was amazing to me, the idea that each of those gravestones, each of the people in the town, had their own poem. It was such a democratic principle, and it changed the way I thought about other people as well as writing. I would meet new people and wonder about their lives not just as stories as they are so often presented, but as poems. Likewise, I found myself considering events in this way.

Later, the poets who most interested me were more cerebral, dealing more with ideas, for example the idea of absence and presence in Mark Strand's "Keeping Things Whole." So much of the power of that poem has to do with its brevity, so that the focus is kept tight on what "is" and "is not" a possibility.

I majored in philosophy as an undergraduate at Kent, although I took as many English classes as I did philosophy classes. I was especially fond of Søren Kierkegaard, who presented existentialism through "what if" narratives, particularly in *Fear and Trembling*. I was knocked out by Sartre's *Being and Nothingness*, as well as the mental gymnastics of Heidegger. I embraced ambiguity in thinking and writing, and I believe that is one of the reasons I stayed away from traditional narrative and its demands for clarity for so long. Poetry, on the other hand, was often enhanced by uncertainty. So, I wrote poetry, often philosophical, narrative poetry. Plato's *Dialogues* also influenced me, and many of my poems were inspired by things that people, often Betty, said to me. Unsurprisingly, my work included a lot of dialogue, which made the transition to fiction seem more natural.

I admit, I had been mulling over the visiting poet's comments about fiction. I wanted to write bigger and more complicated narratives. I could have written book-length poems, I suppose, but at readings at The Center for Writers at the University of Southern Mississippi, I had been listening to the fiction writers. Some had asked me to take my "poets eye" to their story drafts. As I read them, I found myself translating my own ideas for poems into longer, multi-faceted narratives. I worried about how to move people around in a narrative, but was lucky to be a student at the Center and to work with Rick Barthelme in a workshop that also included Kim Chinquee, Darlin' Neal, Nathan Oates, and so many others. I consider my first story a "mulligan." I've never published it, but it contributed to my later work in a very important way. There was always laughter at the fiction readings, and I tried too hard to make my first story funny. It bombed in workshop (as it should have), but Rick always had one-on-one conferences with writers after their stories were presented. Somehow, he saw through the mess of that story (about a man who gives his wife vibrating underwear for Christmas) and found its heart, my heart. I'll never forget him pointing at one line in the story, a place where the narrator, where I, let my guard down. "Here," he said. "More of this." That bit was honest and emotional, exactly what I'd been trying to cover up with extraneous passages about Santa Claus and Christmas cookies. I had been afraid to expose my narrator, myself. What Rick perceived was the thing I had been trying to repress. *I can do that*, I thought. *I can do that all day.* It was as if he could hear the voice in my head, the real story. After that, I tried to listen for that voice myself, to let it speak, not shout, to say just the "thing," whatever it was, and let it rest. Soon, I found myself a "convert" to fiction.

My first short stories were generally comprised of two or three separate strands of narrative. Either thread could have stood alone as a flash, but they were more powerful woven together. Over time, I discovered that the stronger the character, the less likely I was to need more than one story strand. I originally thought of those stories as "concentrate." Later, after I'd written several, I learned they were called "flash." The first one was about a ten-year-old girl who hates her grandfather. The emotion filled up nine hundred words. Nothing more was necessary.

When I started writing about Betty, I found the emotions between the narrator and Betty to be huge. In a novel, they would have been overwhelming and the character and vastness of feeling could have muddled the story line. I wrote one, then two "Betty stories." At the end of each, I felt a very real sense of ending, although I knew more could be said. I found myself pulled in by Betty and her tales, often losing my initial plot completely to follow Betty wherever she wanted to take me. For a while, every time I sat down to write—and some of these were only written because I wanted to write, as opposed to having some agenda—Betty showed up. She could be difficult, demanding, and shinier than I liked. Luckily her visits were brief: flashes. She said what she came to say and left.

At first I fought the way that Betty took over, but eventually, after I caught my breath and had a chance to stand back and take a good look, I welcomed her. On the rare occasion she didn't come to me knowing what she wanted to say, the Betty in "Dragon Lady" became the road map for the flashes. Anything I needed to know about Betty was there.

The separation of both her character and her biography into distinct, individual flashes gave me—and hopefully, the reader—space to breathe. The tension inherent to the novella-in-flash form—that stringing of short pieces into a longer, cohesive one—also kept me from over-thinking the narrative and from over-writing it. I needed there to be a sense of satisfaction at the conclusion of each piece. Each piece demanded its own moment of clarity. As a writer, I needed the space that exists between the ending of one flash and the beginning of another, even if they connect up later, as they do in the novella, so that I could disentangle myself from the writing. However, there was always a thread I could pull to go back to Betty.

The individual Betty stories are never neat, but they fell into place perfectly in the novella. I must have had it in my head, because they cohered easily into an order I never had to question or tweak. Almost of their own accord, the flashes formed a natural arc. I didn't write them in order, but the order was intrinsically there. I wrote other, longer stories about Betty, but they never belonged with the flashes. The only real change I had to make to any part of the novella was to cut about 250 words from the title story. Flash and novella both require a light touch. They demand the discipline to know when to stop, and to recognize the shape. Fortunately, writing poetry had taught me to think in "lines," to remove unnecessary pronouns, to resist the allure of adjectives and adverbs, to let the actions, thoughts, dialogue, or descriptions stand on their own.

Writing flash and novella together reminds me of something I read once about sculpting, that a sculptor can see the sculpture in a rock and simply chips away until the form emerges. I didn't want the character or the story to be lost to the stone. I tried my best to chip away until both could emerge but nothing was lost. Outside the self-contained world of *Betty Superman*, there are other Betty stories that are, because they need to be, longer. I still write Betty poems. I can envision both other Betty projects as full-length collections. Only now that I'm used to her can I imagine Betty loose in a novel, although I cannot promise that it would be pretty. The flashes that make up *Betty Superman* don't belong to a novel, a book of poetry, or a short story collection. *Betty Superman* the novella-in-flash walked out of the stone. I would have been a fool to try to shape the flashes, the novella, into something bigger, longer, or more beautiful.

I believe that every subject makes obvious its own form. I just try to pay attention.

—TIFF HOLLAND

BETTY SUPERMAN

BY TIFF HOLLAND

This book is dedicated to my mother, Polly

TABLE OF CONTENTS

DRAGON LADY

WHAT SHE WEARS: SWEATERS, tight over missile-silo brassieres.
Pink. Yellow. Two pairs of support hose and open-toed shoes,
even in winter. Estée Lauder perfume. Frills. Too much
hairspray on her cotton candy hair. Make-up, every minute
she is awake. False teeth. She had her real ones pulled when
she was twenty. All of them. They were crooked. Then she
tore up all the pictures of herself, all the sweater-girl pictures
of herself in poodle skirts, smiling with her own teeth.
Sometimes, at work, she wears a smock covered in little
pieces of hair. Sometimes the hair sticks to her, her arms and
neck and face. Sometimes it takes root, grows.

What she says: you look like a boy. Chest out! You read too
much. Just a minute, can't you see I'm on the phone? All girls
who play sports are lesbians. Football players are a bunch of
fanny patters. Oh, sit on my lap, you know you want to: you're
Mommy's little girl. Don't frown, you'll get wrinkles. You could
be beautiful if you wanted to. I wish I'd never had you heathens.
Your father? He's in there, lying down, wishing he was dead.
He wants to kill himself. Suicide, get it? It's our fault. He hates
us. Don't make me hit you. Go to the store, here's a note, get me
two packs of Pall Mall. Marlboro. Merit. Give me a kiss, you'll
be sorry if I die during the night. Then you'll miss your mother.

What she calls my friends: losers, lesbians, perverts. What she calls us: heathens, knot-heads, hair-brains, you damn kids. Crazy-makers. Ingrates. Little... She gives us all new names: Applejack for the brother who doesn't stop eating; Neil Armstrong for the smaller, thin and pale; Milquetoast for my father. I'm Milan. She makes us have tea parties, scoop jam out of tiny jars onto overdone toast, make small talk about our imaginary lives.

What she likes: loud music. She turns on my Goodwill stereo early in the morning and dances around, telling me *Rise and shine,* while she twists the volume: up, up, up. She likes to talk on the phone. Do her nails. She thinks the firemen at the station across the street are watching her, making fun of her. Candy bars. Every night she gets up at two or three a.m. and eats a Milky Way, drinks a Coke. I listen. Once she invited me down, too. I wait.

What she does: with switches, Hot Wheels tracks, hair-brushes, shoes—once with a coffee cup. She cries, every day for months, then she stops. She reads us German folk tales. The little boy doesn't wash his hair and small animals live in it. Another boy sucks his thumbs and the great tall tailor comes and cuts them off. She gets religion, drags us, walking through mud puddles, to church on Sunday mornings. She takes up crafts. We make toilet paper drums with felt and glitter for the Christmas tree. We string yarn through burlap sacks, glue macaroni to boards, we shellac at the kitchen table. She goes back to work, leaves us with him. He takes us to McDonald's for lunch, puts the phone in the freezer in case she calls. When someone calls for me, she tells him, tells her, I'm not there. She asks my first boyfriend if I wouldn't be pretty if I gussied up. I hit her back. She asks another boyfriend if he's gay. She asks if I'm a lesbian. She walks in on me in the bathroom and accuses me of masturbating. She smokes. She gets a crush on a local politician. When Dad finally leaves, she tells me it's my fault.

How she is now: she wonders why we aren't close, like we used to be. I tell her we never were, not for a minute. When I try to kill myself, she asks, *How could you do this to me?* She still kisses me, once on each cheek, and rubs the lipstick in. She denies the book of German folk tales. She tells me I need to adopt a baby, be a foster mother, get rid of those stinking dogs. She tells me to put my chest out. Asks, *Do you still love your husband? Really?* She makes me ask my brother if he's gay. He tells me he's not. A few months later, he brings his boyfriend by. She is jealous of my father. You've made him into a saint since he died, she tells me, both of you. She has emphysema, quits smoking. She coughs so hard she wets herself, so hard I know she's going to die and I feel ten again, sitting outside her bedroom door listening to her sleep because she has threatened to die in the night. She ignores me, me breathing each breath with her. She pushes away the napkin I pass across the table. When she recovers, she sucks on a fake cigarette, hard. She rubs it in ash between inhalations. She points it at me across the kitchen table, and I lean back, away from her, in my chair.

HOT WORK

THE TRANSVESTITES LIKE SCARVES although none of the women in the shop wear them, not anymore. The transvestites are slippers-in, after closing. They're incognito in the back room and emerge sweaty flowers. It is hot work, being beautiful, but they are willing to make the concessions, to pay cash so their wives cannot track their other lives. They try on the wigs gathering dust on the top shelves, the ones the beauty shop ladies spurn. It is just them and us, although they would like nothing more than to mingle under the dryers, to nibble donuts and discuss the *National Enquirer*. My mother applies their make-up. I feign sleep in the shampoo chair, sneaking a peek at the finished products: unwinged angels with five o'clock shadows, tottering in circles between the dryers and the styling chairs, trying in that small space to learn how to fly.

BETTY SUPERMAN

WHEN I WAS SEVENTEEN, I had this poster in my room. It was a picture poem by Kenneth Patchen. I didn't know who he was yet, that he was a poet from my very end of the universe. The artwork, the painting part of it, wasn't very well done. I didn't know that was because Patchen could hardly move when he did it, that the last years of life he pretty much wrote from bed. No, I just liked what it said— "All at Once Is What Eternity Is"—which seemed right to my seventeen-year-old mind, explained it all to me the way that nothing else did. I matted the poster in art class and put it in a frame over my bed. Betty hated the poster.

Betty was my mom but I refused to call her that. Even my dad called her "Betty" that year.

"That's got to be the ugliest thing I've ever seen," she told me one morning. She had come into my room to play my Goodwill stereo, even though I was asleep. The stereo was at least ten years old, big and blue with an eight-track player and big globe speakers on pedestals.

I groaned and rolled over, but she pulled the blanket off my bed and began dancing around my room with it like some harlot, twirling, wrapping and unwrapping the blanket around her. I closed my eyes hard and tried to pretend she wasn't there.

I don't remember what LP she had on the turntable. Knowing Betty, it could have been anything, Motown or some soundtrack, Barry Manilow or Barbra Streisand. I remember that year she had a thing for Streisand's "Superman" song. I remember the picture on the cover of that album: Barbra in a white t-shirt with a big "S" on it. Barbra was tugging the shirt down on the cover and looking shyly at the camera. Maybe she wasn't wearing any underwear; maybe that was why she was tugging on that shirt. At the time, I don't think I even noticed. In any case, obviously, neither Betty nor Barbra knew anything about Superman, although even I had to admit Barbra had a set of pipes and so did Betty, and Betty knew it. Whatever was playing that morning and every other morning for that matter, Betty sang along. "Porgy I'se your womaannnn..." she'd sing from *Porgy and Bess* or dirty stuff by Barry White. She sang all day long, and it wouldn't have been so bad if she could have kept the lyrics straight. But each song was a sort of mosaic of every song she knew with Porgy sneaking into Superman and Elvis intruding on "Stayin' Alive." I remember how disappointed I was, years later, when I learned that Neil Diamond had not written a song about "Reverend Blue Jeans" but "Forever in Blue Jeans." Eventually she vacated my room and I turned off the stereo.

She made breakfast that day. Afterwards, I went back to bed to sleep some more. That was one of my favorite things when I was seventeen, napping after breakfast, but

Betty had to ruin that, too. I devoured the cinnamon rolls and sausages and carried what was left of my juice back up to my room. I'd just drifted off when I heard the sound of pebbles plunking against the window. It was Betty. She had on her gardening hat and gloves and was holding a basket of tiger lilies she must have just cut.

"What?!" I demanded, throwing open the window.

"What light through yonder window breaks!" Betty shouted.

"Huh?"

"I said, what light through yonder window breaks," Betty repeated, "and you're supposed to say..."

She paused for a moment. I looked around the neighborhood to see if anyone was watching. I couldn't have been more embarrassed if Betty was wearing a Superman outfit.

"You're supposed to say..." Betty continued and paused again.

"All at Once Is What Eternity Is!" I shouted.

"Oh, come on, play nice. You'll wish you'd played along after you leave home." Betty took off her hat and put down the basket. "You know the rest."

But I didn't. I had no use for Shakespeare at seventeen. I took the glass of juice off the nightstand, took aim, and let it pour down on Betty's head. She screamed and jumped and looked up to yell at me just as the glass slipped from my hand. I like ice in my juice, and the condensation must have made it slippery. It tumbled in slow motion down to Betty where it conked her right between the eyes. She fell to the ground.

I'd never run down those stairs so fast. The glass was

intact, to my surprise, but had left a large gash on Betty's forehead, kind of above her eyes, the place she was always warning me I was going to get wrinkles if I didn't stop frowning. She was on her butt on the grass and calmly reached over and put her hat back on her head.

"Let me see, Mom," I pleaded.

"No," she sounded like a child, "you didn't want to play."

"Look, we have to get that looked at," I told her. Blood was trickling down the bridge of her nose. I took her hand to lead her to the car.

"Ehh, ehh, ehh," Betty clucked, "you say your line first."

"It is the sun and thou art the moon?" I guessed.

Betty thought for a minute. She still couldn't remember the line. She let me pull her to her feet.

"Ok, but no more of that eternity crap," she admonished.

"Ok," I agreed. She followed me a few feet.

"Wait! Wait! My flowers!"

"They'll be fine," I assured her.

She sang most of the way to the hospital. I tried turning on the radio to drown her out, but she just sang along, mangling the words as usual, until she fell asleep.

FIRST HUSBAND

MY MOTHER, WEARING BRIGHT COLORS as always, and with something snappy blaring on the stereo, swings open the door. Mike is five-four although he claims five-six, and he's holding a small bouquet of grocery store flowers. I've warned him about my mother.

"My, aren't you queery looking?" she says.

"These are for you."

He thrusts the wilty flowers into her hand and strides down the hall, his footsteps clacking because he wears those short boots he likes. My second husband will call them "Beatle Boots." My first husband just calls them Florsheims. I call them dorky, but in any case, he isn't fazed.

I am standing at the end of the hall underneath a sort of mini-chandelier, which is missing two of its dangling prisms. It is the chandelier my best friend Tracy once swung from, giving my mother fits, and I believe this incident has made it the most powerful spot in the house.

"Ready?" he asks.

My mother is coming after him, but I am already ready. I have been ready all my life. She says something as we pass, but I can't hear her. I told her we're going to a haunted house, but really, we're going shooting. That would really drive her nuts. I can't believe my eyes when we get to the lake and he pops the trunk to reveal guns, a variety: pistols and rifles and a shotgun. I will wonder what I am doing. I met Mike Brown working at a pizza parlor. He hasn't yet joined the Army. I have never been this close to any form of weaponry. Even the knives in our house are dull.

When I come home, the flowers will be in a vase in my bedroom, a plain glass vase with a chip on the top. My mother will have put them there to make a point, but I won't care. I will have shot pine cones and empty RC Cola cans (the preferred beverage at the Brown household) to pieces. I will have shredded lily pads with buckshot and amazed my future husband. I will have discovered a talent I didn't know I had. I am a hell of a shot. Already it will have occurred to me, I could always shoot her.

THE RED SNAPPER

she told me the truth.

"Your Great Aunt Leone? Lesbian."

She put the oxygen mask up to her mouth and inhaled as if she were taking a hit, lowered it.

"We walked in on her one time, with Cousin Linda in the back room. You remember Cousin Linda…" She slipped off for a moment into a side narrative about this cousin I never knew, but I waited. I had learned to be patient.

"They were in there together in bed, Linda suckin' one of Leone's titties. Why, we didn't know what to do, just stood there. I think Cassie screamed and Mama yelled back at Linda to cut it out, for Leone to button up."

I'd never heard her call my grandmother "Mama" before, I was certain of that, although I couldn't remember what she did call her—"The Old Girl," maybe. That sounded right. I was trying to think of ways to remember this story, this story she told me not to tell before she remembered I couldn't remember any more, that all her stories were safe with me now.

"What about Uncle Ed?" I asked. "I mean, if she was a lesbian…"

"Well, bi-sexual," she stretched the word out. "Whatever. You know."

She looked. I knew the look. She wanted an ashtray. Even though she'd stopped smoking, had to, she still looked for an ashtray at times like this. She sipped her coffee. There was only a smudge of lipstick left. Most of it was smeared on the oxygen mask.

"Leone was stacked. You remember that?" She started back up. "What a bosom."

I could still see pictures in my mind. Leone was red there, red outfits, red lipstick, an overbite, all her outfits straining across the chest. I nodded. I asked about the teeth. It seemed odd that Leone had such bucky teeth. Meanwhile, I searched in my back pocket for a piece of paper, found the receipt from lunch. I didn't remember paying or shoving the slip in my pocket, but it was how I usually handled things. There were usually notes in my pockets to remind me of things, notes I wrote on neon-colored paper so they would catch my attention. The pen the waitress had left still sat on the table.

"Oh, well, Ed made her get those. He picked them out. She was too pretty, so he picked the ugliest dentures he could find. Didn't fit good either." She sounded winded. "Didn't stop her." Mom chuckled.

"One time I saw her walkin' the tracks, just swayin', talkin' to herself. She was havin' an affair with Jimmy Brown, you know. Mama loved him so, but Leone couldn't help herself. Anyway, she was drunk as a skunk and walkin' back home after a nooner with him. That's what you call it, right? She stumbled between those rails. Cacklin'! I could hear her comin' but I never said anything. Your grandmother always said she gave Leone and Barb her leftovers, but Leone took 'em. She could have any man she wanted." Mom started coughing, hard. I waited a minute, handed her the mask, then slid the pen over the table and into my lap while she inhaled, closing her eyes. Under the table I scribbled notes. I wasn't sure I'd be able to read them later.

A DISAPPEARING POPULACE

MY MOTHER KEEPS HER MONEY in a Pringles can. She used to use a Benefiber jar, but then her husband got all healthy and found her stash so she switched places.

"That man is trouble," she tells me, "always snooping about." But he's mom's third, and she's ready, always ready to bail, to put him out on the pavement.

When he threatens to leave she tells him: put the mailbox key on the table. She doesn't care anymore. She spends her days watching *Desperate Housewives*, cackling. She only goes out when Three is at work. That way she doesn't have to worry.

About two every afternoon, she makes a trip to McDonald's for coffee and stops at Walgreens for candy bars. She has subsisted on these items for almost three years now, although tonight she is cooking eggs and fried potatoes for Three. His request. She doesn't care. He's still jealous. She sits in front of him with a plate and the candy bar. She cuts it carefully into bites as if it were a steak. She brings the fork to her mouth slowly before gobbling each bite like Godzilla consuming the populace of Tokyo. Then she wipes, daintily, and takes another bite.

THE BARBERTON MAFIA

THE FIRST TIME SHE TOLD ME THE STORY, he was a pimp.
I remember the word "pimp." How could someone forget
that? If my entire slate had been wiped clean, I would
remember the word "pimp" the way I remember the word
"orgasm," the way she first said it to me, on the phone—
probably so she wouldn't have to look at me—the way she
lowered her voice. "Tony" was his name, and I remember
that, too. She and my father were separated, but it still felt
like cheating to me, my father's daughter, dark like him
and book smart the way Mom never was. She said she
should have stayed with this Tony, although then I would
never have been born. She said she thought he may have
been her one true love.

But now, when I ask her about the other things she has
said that she will not—should not—tell me, I ask about
Tony. We are driving down 620 to Walgreens. I am
driving. Six months ago it was the other way around. I
was sicker. She drove while I gave directions. Today, she is
coughing in the passenger seat, occasionally spitting into
a tissue she has pulled from inside her bra. Once again, she
has refused to bring her portable oxygen.

"So, you said you didn't want to tell me any more. That

some of it is just too bad, and I'm wondering: what, what could be that bad?" I ask. Remembering the last bit, about my Great Aunt Leone, because I took notes, because I found the words "lesbian," "tittie," and "dentures" on a receipt that I almost threw away. "I mean, you said Leone was a lesbian, big deal, and I know about Michael Todd and..." There was something else. That I forgot.

"Your father was mean to me. He was so mean."

"Okay."

"Even his own mother said I should leave him."

The floors of my childhood were covered in the ceramic shards of broken knick-knacks. Once, we crawled through a window to escape him pounding on a bedroom door. We shared secrets before she started telling me. I look out the window at a group of buzzards feasting on a small deer by the side of the road. In this part of Texas the deer are small but plentiful. I put on my turn signal.

"So," I say. "Tony."

"Oh, he was good to me. So good to me. He was I-talian." She always stretches out that word, elongates the vowel. I envision a dark-skinned man dressed like the narc from *Starsky and Hutch*, Chicken or Rooster something. I wonder if this Tony wore a hat.

"He took me nice places. He gave me things."

He didn't break them, I think.

"Anyway, your father and I made up."

I pull up near the door. Mom still hasn't completed the paperwork for her handicapped placard, although I can see the top of it sticking out of her purse. Maybe, like me, she thinks if she holds out she'll get better. I did.

"He was a pimp?"

"Oh, I don't know. He always had lots of pretty girls around him. But then…okay, I think he was Mafia."

She pushes used tissues into the trash bag that hangs from the lighter nub, then grabs fresh tissues from a box on the floor and shoves them into her bra. I know for a fact that at any given moment the bra is home to several tissues, her asthma inhaler, roughly thirty dollars in cash and one or two hard candies. I imagine her loading it up in the mornings the way my husband loads his pockets.

"Mafia? The Barberton Mafia? There's Mafia in Barberton?"

My mother's hometown is tiny, with a small, perfectly round man-made lake in the center of town. That's really about it.

"I don't know. Maybe Cleveland."

She arranges her purse on her elbow, reaches for the door handle. I get out and walk around in case she needs help, but she's good. Inside she makes sure I get a cart, so I can lean on it if I have to. She leans on hers. I abandon mine as soon as she's out of sight. No one in Cleveland goes to Barberton, not for anything. I shove my hands in my pockets. I'm careful not to look at anything too carefully. The aisles, the rows of products, and fluorescent lights are overwhelming. I get tired quickly and look for her in the candy aisle. She has a box of Russell Stover's and sixteen candy bars. She frowns when she notices I'm cart-less.

"I didn't want to buy anything," I say.

She looks at the MedicAlert bracelet on my wrist but keeps quiet.

"You done?" I ask.

"Yes. It's time for my treatment."

We stop at McDonald's on the way back. Every day at three, she has a cup of McDonald's coffee.

"So, did he have a gun?" I ask, waiting as the minivan moms in the vans ahead of us pass Happy Meal after Happy Meal back to children watching cartoons on built-in DVD players.

"Tony? I don't know. I suppose."

But that doesn't tell me anything. Mafia, pimp—both would do well to have a gun.

"And you just went back to Dad?"

She is peering inside her bag, checking to make sure she has the requested four creams. She gives a nod, and I pull away from the window.

"I went back. He promised to be better, to stop drinking, and he did."

"But you still wish you'd stayed with this Tony?"

"I didn't say that."

"You didn't?"

It's amazing how much progress the buzzards have made in such a short time. The deer's ribs are clean and crows sit on the barbed wire, waiting for the big birds to finish, so they can have their turn.

STRETCHED

MOM'S NOT ALL THE WAY IN THE CAR when she asks if she
ever told me she had her pee-hole stretched.

"Uh, no," I answer, nodding to remind her Lauren is
in the backseat as Mom swings her other leg in, sets her
purse on her lap, and pulls hard at the door. You'd think it
was made of concrete.

I have the air on all the way because it helps Mom
breathe. I pointed all the vents in her direction before we
left the house.

"Anyway," Mom starts back up and I open my eyes big
and nod again back at Lauren, but Mom says, "She's not
paying attention."

"Oh yes she is."

I adjust the mirror to look at Lauren more carefully. She is
paying way too much attention to her handheld video game.

"Oh well." Mom waves her hand and tells me how it had
to be stretched, and asks if I was living in Hawaii or maybe
Mississippi or where when it was done?

"How do I know? This is the first I've heard of it."

I check carefully behind the car as I back out. I have to
concentrate extra hard with other people in the car. I have
extra blind spots, but I know where they are.

"I think that's when they found the extra pouch on my bladder, too."

I have heard about the extra pouch. Mom says Aunt Muff has one, too, but I never called to ask. This all seems too personal to me.

"Mom, can we talk about something else? I don't think Lauren needs to hear this."

"Well, I was thinking maybe hers needs stretched, too. She doesn't pee near enough."

I pull up at the apartment gate and wait for it to slide and let us out. Mom is quiet while I wait for the left onto O'Conner, which is crazy busy, and by the time we hit the light at 620 she's lost her train of thought, started telling me some other story, something about the old ladies in the building. But she remembers it when we're seated at the Cracker Barrel, where I order for her because she drives the waitresses crazy.

"She'd like her eggs over medium," I tell a young woman with freckles. "She likes a little yolk, but not too runny and no crunchy brown stuff on the edges." I raise my eyebrows when I speak so the waitress knows I think it's too much but could she just indulge Mom, for my sake.

"No problem," the girl answers and takes up the menus. Lauren will have chicken fingers. I'll have the special. I always do, because it's getting too hard to actually read the menu and everything here tastes the same. Mom is halfway through her eggs when she remembers the pee-hole.

"Did you have to have surgery?" I ask, taking a bite of a corn muffin.

"No, I think he did it in the office."

"Really? That sounds surgical to me. Didn't you need anesthesia?"

I'm beginning to reconsider encouraging her to tell me her secrets. I used to just tune her out or change the subject, especially when we were eating. Now I hear about pee-holes and her first orgasm and about how someone dug up the family burial ground.

"I don't remember. It hurt like hell."

"I bet it did."

I look at Lauren. Usually she would be giggly at any mention of "pee." I can only assume she really has tuned us out—or she's worried we might have it done to her. In any case, she asks to go to the bathroom when she's done eating. I stand outside the door, listening to a stream of water hitting the bowl hard for a long time. When we come out, Mom is at the register paying, telling the cashier how perfect her eggs were and how nice the waitress was. I slip back to the table and throw down another three bucks for the tip to make it an even five.

SELF-SERVE UNLEADED

ON THE WAY TO SELL OUR GOLD FOR CASH, we stopped for gas. Mom had been telling me things again, secrets, not-so secrets: double cousins who married and molesting uncles, how my favorite uncle back home wouldn't take blood thinners because he didn't want to stop drinking beer. The last time I saw him he looked pregnant. It was his liver. He started getting dizzy screwing in light bulbs. He had all his teeth pulled and the false ones clacked.

"Sorry, I have to stop."

I had ten bucks left for gas and planned to use the gold money to fill the tank enough to get me to my first payday at the end of the month. I didn't like filling the tank with Mom in the car. Gas fumes are bad for asthmatics, but it wasn't too hot a day, low on the ozone meter.

"You know I've never pumped gas," Mom said.

"You're kidding me," I said, looking at her as I put the car into park.

"Never? Not even once? In an emergency?"

"No, never." She seemed proud of it.

I hit the electric window buttons. All four windows went down at once. It was breezy, cool.

"Maybe some day you could teach me?" She seemed genuinely interested.

"You're not messing with me?" I tend to mess around like that, to make false admissions, see how people take it. I do it all the time with Mom. She shook her head vigorously.

"Hmm."

Sometimes I had my students do "procedural writing"—write how to do an everyday activity in the smallest detail. Pumping gas was a favorite.

I turned the engine off.

"You always have to turn it off," I said.

Mom looked at me closely.

"And you can't smoke while you do it. It's dangerous."

She nodded.

I opened the door.

"In this car you have to pull up on this little tab to open the gas door, the tiny door near the back." I exaggerated pulling up the tab and gestured toward the back of the car like a game show assistant. Mom kept watching.

"Then you swipe your debit card," I showed her the magnetic stripe, and slid it through the reader.

"I don't have one of those."

"You don't have a debit card?"

"No, and I don't want one."

"Well, you can pay cash. You have to go inside. There's usually a button. Sometimes it's big and red and you push it and tell the attendant how much you want."

"Okay, I'll do that."

"Fine. Then you unscrew the cap. You can't lose it. They're all attached to the hole these days." Again, I demonstrated. "Choose your grade. Just pick the lowest number and make sure you look. Sometimes, they try to trick you into picking the more expensive one, but they're all the same. Says so in *Consumer Reports*."

Mom was craning her neck. Watching closely. After my stroke, I had forgotten how to pump gas. The first time I had to do it, I thought of my students' papers. I pulled at the small square door. I looked all over for a way to open it, and finally I found the tab.

"Then you put the nozzle in the hole. Voilà!"

"That's it?"

"That's it."

"I think I can do that."

"I'm sure you can, and if you have any trouble you just call the attendant."

The gas started to whoosh through the hose. I cleaned all the tissues from behind the front seat, keeping a close eye on the total.

I looked around for the attendant button. It wasn't there. I ran my hands over the soft pushy buttons on the face of the machine. It seemed like touching things helped me read sometimes. Mom continued to watch closely. The digital numbers clicked to one-zero point zero-zero and I removed the hose. Then I saw the button, just over the handicap call button. I had forgotten about those handicap call buttons.

"Or," I opened the door. "You can push the handicap button." I was relieved—there was no way Mom could walk up to the station, pay, walk back, and pump. It would be way too much for her, but she had the placard.

"You hit that blue button. They'll ask if you need help and come out and pump it."

"Really?"

"They should. I think it's one of those accessibility laws. Just make sure you pump during the day."

I couldn't believe I'd forgotten the stupid button. Mom turned toward the front.

"Well then, I'll never have to pump it."

"Guess not. Shouldn't."

I turned the key. Mom brought out a big bag of gold jewelry. I had a knotted bracelet in my pocket and a skinny, twirly chain too small for my neck.

"Good," Mom said, settling the bag in her lap. I could almost see her forgetting everything I'd just said.

HOMING

I'M NOT AFRAID OF THE COUGH ANYMORE. It's worse now, sure. Sometimes, it sounds like cats fighting, bad plumbing. Lately, it doesn't sound like any one thing and nothing natural, but Mom says it doesn't hurt. She pulls inhalers from her bra the way a magician pulls silk scarves from his mouth. Sometimes, Mom spits up a little into one of the Kleenexes she also keeps in her bra. Her face goes red. She can't speak, but she says it doesn't hurt. She exhales before she puts the inhaler to her lips, leaving room for the medicine when she inhales. Watching her is how I finally figured out how to smoke pot, but she's okay afterwards, a little hoarse, but okay, and this cough, some version of it, is the way I've found her for almost thirty years, in the aisles of the Acme or the Salvation Army. It's a sort of radar, each hack seemingly louder as I close in.

She's had a good day. Lunch at Cracker Barrel. Shoes for Lauren at Payless and now a final trip to Walgreens. The shopping cart is a prophylactic, something to lean on if she starts up again. She tries to get me to take one, too, in case I lose my balance, but I'm feeling cocky.

I head down the card aisle because it's the farthest to the left from the entrance, excepting cosmetics. I have no interest in cosmetics and I always travel left to right. Mom wheels away toward the middle. She's in her red outfit: red capris, red v-neck t-shirt, and long-sleeved red t-shirt over it so no one can see her arms. I've worked my way down to sinus medications when she starts coughing. Nothing major. I head up to paperbacks, try to make out the titles with those first two letters missing, the ones I can't get back. Language is forgiving. I fill in the blanks. I figure there's nothing I want to read, but I like looking at the covers, picking them up, feeling the raised surface of the smallest paperbacks, wondering why the publishers do that, raise the lettering or the outline of the cover art. I like being able to get close to things, not to have the cart or a walker between me and everything else.

In the meantime, the coughing has gotten worse, constant and bark-like, but nothing like the noises I've heard her make just sitting at the kitchen table, struggling to pull the phlegm up the knots of her scarred bronchi. So, I'm surprised to see her between candy and magazines with a circle of people forming around her, lifting their arms to hold hands.

"Is it okay if we pray for you?" a man asks. He's wearing khakis and a short-sleeved button-down, glasses. Beside him is an older woman in a "World's Best Grandma" t-shirt and on the other side a teenage boy with a buzzcut in jeans and a UT shirt. Mom continues to cough, louder and more desperately. They lower their heads without waiting for an answer.

I walk toward them as fast as I can, the products on the shelf blurring with movement. Stores make me dizzy. I should have been more cautious or stayed with her. Up close, Mom's eyes are big and round like a caught animal, and I can see she's trying to get the inhaler out before they open their eyes back up, before they catch her with her hand down her shirt.

I feel the stumble before it's out of control. I have time to correct, but I don't. I let myself sway into the shelf enough to knock down a few boxes of Russell Stover's so that when the impromptu prayer group looks up, it's at me, and not at Mom, who has managed to pull the emergency inhaler out and exhale and then inhale deeply. I pull myself upright before the group can encircle me.

"I'm good," I say as they help put the boxes on the shelf. Back in the car I can't tell if she's been laughing or crying; her face is wet and red and she dabs at it with more Kleenex, still out of breath from her escape.

"Did they pray for you, too?" she asks, reaching behind me to shove a handful of used tissues into the trash bag behind the front seat. By the time I drop her at her garage, the coughing has stopped entirely and she remembers the abandoned cart.

"Darn it. Now I don't have anything sweet."

But I know she does—some kind of cake or cookie is always in her fridge or on the countertop. I offer to go back.

"They don't have the ones I really like anyway. Fast Break. So hard to find and when you do they're never fresh. Next time I'm going to the gas station. They're better there."

She hits the button on her key chain and the garage door

goes up. She leans over to kiss me, thanks me for driving. She doesn't rub the lipstick in the way she used to even when I was in my thirties, and I don't rub it away either.

ABOUT THE AUTHOR

TIFF HOLLAND is originally from Ohio. She attended The Center for Writers at the University of Southern Mississippi. Her poetry, fiction, and creative nonfiction appear regularly in literary magazines and anthologies and have won several awards. Her novella-in-flash *Betty Superman* won the Rose Metal Press Fifth Annual Short Short Chapbook Contest in 2011. She has taught creative writing and literature at Kent State, University of Southern Mississippi, and Austin Community College. She currently lives in Hawaii.

2 | MEG POKRASS

Breaking the Pattern to Make the Pattern:
Conjuring a Whole Narrative from Scraps

Here, Where We Live

BREAKING THE PATTERN TO MAKE THE PATTERN:
CONJURING A WHOLE NARRATIVE FROM SCRAPS

"There is no greatness where there is not simplicity, goodness, and truth."

—LEO TOLSTOY

IF YOU ASK AN ARTIST WHO CREATES crazy quilts how they come up with their designs, that artist will likely tell you that each finished project originates from an emotional place. Each quilt is different because it is made of many found scraps and pieces of cloth in different sizes with no regular color or pattern—the sleeves of an old work shirt, perhaps, or the skirt of a wedding dress. Similarly, the writing of a novella-in-flash involves working with flash fiction fragments and stories by linking them together to form a layered, narrative arc. Working in both art forms demands an improvisational spirit regarding the creation of both content and structure. A novella-in-flash writer and a crazy quilt artist both become familiar with navigating incompletion and juxtaposition.

Both art forms involve delving into the most unlikely places and finding pieces which, when put together, create an untraditional whole. The aim of a novella-in-flash is to create chapters that can stand alone as individual stories, while at the same time moving the narrative toward the larger, overall story arc. Just as a crazy quilt artist takes the time to prepare and stitch each patch, the flash pieces are written and polished as independent stories.

My novella-in-flash *Here, Where We Live* was born out of many of my poems and stories from the last twenty years. I conceptualized the storyline by beginning with older pieces that had been collecting dust in my metaphorical scrap bag. I had written stories and poems over the years involving a teenage girl and her mother—stories that felt in some way connected. It excited me that while searching for and gathering up my old writings, new ideas began to form in my mind about the narrative arc for *Here, Where We Live* and the significant characters began to take shape. As I stitched the stories together, the juxtapositions brought with them fresh energy and new meaning.

Beginning with the two female characters from my older stories, my process for piecing together the structure for *Here, Where We Live* was a little unusual. I had written another novella-in-flash the year before and ultimately decided the entire ending of that book didn't work for that particular narrative. But the ending worked in other ways and became the inspiration point for building *Here, Where We Live*. I began working my way forward from that lost ending. Finding my narrative arc involved imagining what might happen when so much goes wrong in a young person's life, exploring how she might cope with various stresses and joys, and especially, how she might contain within herself the contrasting qualities of wisdom—born of hardship—and the stubborn immaturity of a teenager.

While writing *Here, Where We Live* I looked to many of my older fragments and poems to guide me. A crazy quilt may be made of scraps of silk, velvet, wool, cotton, and linen. Bits of a family wedding suit might be sewn next to a patch of fabric from a childhood toy, and both may be next to a just-discovered piece of fabric. Similarly, writing the novella-in-flash involved integrating pre-existing flashes and giving them a home surrounded by new neighbors—an entirely unexpected new order that ends up feeling just right.

If you look at the Beatles' album *Abbey Road*, for example, and notice the order of the songs, you'll discover how each song as been placed before or after the others to create a unique overall effect. With *Abbey Road*, considered by many critics to be one of the best rock albums ever created, each song is individually stunning. Yet what brings the listener to her knees is the way "I Want You (She's So Heavy)" comes right before "Here Comes the Sun," which is followed by "Because" and on and on. The brilliance is in the way each song is placed—sad followed by happy, followed by funny, followed by strange. You never really know what is coming around the bend, and even when you do know, it is surprising again, retaining—because of its careful ordering—the ability to strike the listener anew. Like songs in an album, each chapter of the novella-in-flash must feel whole and strong so as to enhance the overall feeling and to bear up under repeated readings and re-readings.

Two books that reward this kind of sustained and repeated attention and that influenced my love for this form were written before the term "flash fiction" existed: *Mrs. Bridge* (1959) and *Mr. Bridge* (1969) by Evan S. Connell. A master at showing the reader just enough, Connell wrote linked vignettes in both of these novels, which allows the reader a window into the lives of his characters. Connell's vignettes, though seemingly uneventful, are a mixture of poignancy and unflinching sadness. At the end of each book, one is left with a strong feeling of having known his characters as though one had lived with them, with the order of the stories contributing heavily to that intimate character encounter.

I'd be remiss if I didn't also mention a film that I admire, one that creates the feeling of an entire life, by showing the audience just a sliver. *Cléo from 5 to 7* is a French film made in 1962 by Agnès Varda. The movie focuses on an anxious hour-and-a-half in the life of a woman as it plays out in real-time while she waits to hear the results of a medical test that will possibly confirm a diagnosis of cancer. Varda shows the audience Cléo's character by focusing on tiny actions and details. As with effective flash fiction, it is the details that haunt the viewer: We see Cléo walking past shop windows and looking at her reflection in the glass, we see her waiting for a visit from her lover, as if for the first time. We see her driving with a girlfriend and trying to feel carefree, the way she felt before she knew she may have a terminal illness. This brief and compact film addresses existentialism, mortality, the nature of despair, and what it is to lead a meaningful life, and proves that a work of art does not need to be long to leave the audience contemplating it for a long time after.

To return to the crazy quilt analogy, these means of compressed and fragmentary, almost scrap-like composition remind both the author and the reader that life unfolds in minutes, hours, and days, weeks and years. Some moments are colorful and brilliant, many are normal or even drab, and others are sad and desperate and misshapen. We humans frequently have very little perspective on our own stories while we are living them. The novella-in-flash, divided into tiny bits of action, mirrors life this way. I do not believe that life as it is being lived has a "narrative arc"—and if it does, it does not become clear until a person is gone.

Bearing this in mind, each time I experimented with the order of this odd assortment of chapters in *Here, Where We Live*, it felt as though the novella could easily take an entirely new direction. This was tricky. My hardest decisions involved defining what felt true and consistent with the characters I was creating. Only after rearranging the order again and again could I define a desirable narrative arc. Next, it was time to write what felt as though were missing. This was like writing connective tissue, or seams to hold the patchwork narrative together.

Unique to this form, the novella-in-flash contains frequent

pauses when chapters end, with each story chapter being under 1,000 words. I've come to see these spaces as where the reader takes a breath, which creates a rhythmic reading experience overall. I enjoyed exploring how breathlessly close to ruin both daughter and mother become in this novella-in-flash. I wanted, as the writer, to have them relive the same issues and themes again and again with sporadic progress, like gasping for breath.

Another book that fostered my desire to attempt my own novella-in-flash is *Why Did I Ever* (2001) by Mary Robison, whose stunning depictions of messy lives are rendered imaginatively by working with tiny fragments assembled together in a way that highlights the way ends and beginnings of chapters can be used to create rhythmic gaps like breathing. Robison wrote *Why Did I Ever* on hundreds of note cards over a long period of time. Some scenes or chapters are only one sentence long, whereas others are a few pages. Robison's white spaces are structurally significant, as they are with my own novella-in-flash, where there are frequent pauses between chapters in which the reader takes a breath and makes the leap from one story to the next, following the threads of narrative mapped out by the author.

After all the patchwork pieces have been found, assembled and reassembled, and sewn together with equal parts seams and gaps, only then does the larger quilt or narrative become clear. As the writer, now I can stand back a bit from *Here, Where We Live* and see exactly where each fragment belonged and how each one contributes to the larger work. And my hope is that the reader will feel equally intrigued when reading the novella—wrapped up in the narrative made of overlaid, stitched-together stories.

—MEG POKRASS

HERE, WHERE WE LIVE

BY MEG POKRASS

For Bobbie Ann Mason and Pamela Painter

TABLE OF CONTENTS

HERE, WHERE WE LIVE

I THINK ABOUT HOW BREASTS are meant to be life-giving forces while peeling oranges at night in Nana's front yard—now our front yard. Since Mom's mastectomy, I miss Pittsburgh more than I did before. People there had character.

At nearly sixteen, my breasts have finally sprouted, yet I feel afraid to touch them. Mom says her lump was the size of a small loquat when she found it. She told me this while we were picking up rotten fruit in the yard.

The yard is full of fruit trees: orange, tangelo, and loquat. "All of this food just going to waste kills me," Mom says. Most of the fruit hangs on the branches half-eaten by birds.

We moved out West a few years ago, after Nana left us her falling-apart house that Mom grew up in. The house used to be pretty nice, but since nobody has taken care of it in what looks like forever, it has become depressing. Relatives thought it would be good for us to move and start over. Dad died working on a hotel restoration project in Pittsburgh and there is too much of him there.

Back East, people were far less attractive but colorful. Some of them were even fat. Here in Santa Barbara people appear bland and predictable as the weather—skinny and blond, walking around in beachwear. Girls with billboard eyes gather at the new mall on State Street, but you can't tell them apart.

"Gotta love living in Perfectland!" Mom says.

SEE YA LATER

WHEN I WANDER INTO THE GARAGE my eyes find Dad's clear plastic bins full of shirts, stacked in a crooked row. They sit next to a few clear boxes full of Mom's old plays and playbills.

I recognize one of Dad's ratty t-shirts, can just see the outline of a wrinkled dog's face pressed into the side of a bin. Mom used to tease him about how he grew so attached to clothes that he wore them until they shredded. I stand by the rows of boxes, saying in my head what Dad used to say to me every time he left for work, and trying not to think about the time he said it but didn't come home again, three years ago now, when I was twelve and almost as tall as I am now. The doctor says I'm done growing.

I say it three times now to make sure he knows I haven't forgotten:

See you later, Abby-gator . . . see you later, Abby-gator. . . see you later, Abby-gator.

Dad fixed old falling apart homes and buildings, so I imagine him plumping up the squashed-in parts of our ceiling, filling in the cracks around the windows.

Mom's boyfriend, Daniel, is no good at fixing stuff. His cologne swells up inside our living room, stinking like the bathroom in a gas station mini-mart, so I open the windows even though it makes Mom put on her thick, ugly sweaters.

SPARKLY PLANS

A FEW MONTHS AFTER CHEMOTHERAPY, Mom got a part-time telemarketing job selling ballet season tickets. She didn't sell enough, though, so they fired her after just three weeks.

Mom said she hated selling people tickets they didn't want. She would tell people not to buy anything over the phone if they sounded old. She was proud of getting fired.

Unemployed, she still sends money to Friends of the Bird Refuge, The Homeless Coalition, and Save the Trees. I worry about where she is finding money to do this. Daniel works, and he lives here rent-free, so I figure they must have some arrangement to even things out.

I look at old photos of Mom from when she was an actress— her hair all modelish, and her eyes full of sparkly plans.

Now she wears hats, scarves, hoop earrings, wigs. But nothing makes her look normal.

The new baby-chick fuzz on Moms' scalp feels so soft that sometimes I pet it and say "nice nice fuzz," but Mom touches her scalp too much. When she does that, even at the beach art show, even where everyone is supposed to be interesting and artsy—even there, she looks like a bald weirdo fingering her head.

GREASE

THE RENAISSANCE FAIRE IS COMING UP in just a few weeks. My best friend Junie's brother Kyle, a few years older, will drive us an hour south, to Agoura Hills. In photos, Kyle doesn't look like anyone interesting.

The Faire is a place where teenagers can roam around without anyone bothering them. This sounds good to me, because lately, older guys have been gawking at my tits, and it makes me feel weird.

Junie says people who don't like attention are gay, which makes no sense, and has nothing to do with anything.

I try not to be mad because Junie is my only friend, and hanging out usually takes my brain off of all the crap at home.

Mom is on a very restrictive diet prescribed by a nutritionist. I'm sick of vegan everything. Our kitchen overflows with unbleached sesame seeds and fake-meat patties made of tofu-turds.

At the Faire, I'll be free to wander around with Junie and eat all the junky food I want.

What I crave most are those huge turkey drumsticks they sell in greasy food carts, the heavy taste of meat fat.

LUCK

ON OUR STOOP, LUCK CLEARS ITS THROAT like a Mormon missionary and walks away.

We can't afford a therapy dog, so we rescue a pound-mutt called Bruno. The dog, though friendly, has a permanently depressed expression. A plastic surgeon would take his downward hanging cheeks and move them up, above his ears.

"I'm sick and tired of it all," Mom says, folding kitchen dish towels. I used to try to help, but apparently, I don't fold towels right.

Our luck is a flat can of open Pepsi left out all night. Normal people would toss it, but Mom never wastes anything.

Sometimes she talks about how I was born with colic, wanted nothing to do with her milk.

"That is you all over," she says.

I imagine Mom whisking soy powder with water, the rise and fall of her functional but useless breasts.

I make a mental list of recent unlucky things:

> —We got a dog who looks sad but was supposed to make us feel happy.
> —Dad died making an old building new.
> —The front of our house is sinking into the ground.

—Daniel and Mom talk about my attitude when they think I can't hear. They say I don't listen, but I'm just trying not to hear the idiotic things Daniel says to Mom.

To protect my luck, I've become good at:

1. Not thinking when it makes things worse.

2. Chopping onions with my eyes squeezed shut.

3. Brightening my nights by moving things along the softest part of my body.

RENAISSANCE FAIRE

ON OUR WAY TO THE RENAISSANCE FAIRE, I catch Junie's brother Kyle looking at me in the car mirror while driving. Daniel does this often, and I'm getting used to hiding my face. Kyle wears a shield of armor made of bicycle parts. It is not at all Medieval-looking—it looks like an ugly piece of welded backyard junk, which is why I like it, and why I believe he did it. But I don't know him well enough to compliment him on it. It's July, hot as hell, and I can't imagine how he will walk around like that.

I'm wearing a t-shirt that says: *The more I learn about people, the more I like my dog. –Mark Twain*

Kyle laughs when he first sees it on me, and I laugh too. Nobody would wear a t-shirt like this to a Medieval festival, which is why I do.

"Pretend we don't know him," Junie said about Kyle once, when we saw him walking near the Bird Refuge. He spends a lot of time alone and he seems obsessed with ducks. To Junie this makes him pathetic. To me it makes him ten times more interesting than Junie.

Kyle's already contributed money by paying for parking at the Faire and the gas to drive us here. I admire Kyle's responsible attitude and his scurrying around to stay out of our way. Maybe Kyle keeps an eye out for Junie because she can be stupidly fearless. This is what I like and don't like about being friends with her.

I want to say to Kyle, "Play dead, why don't you, so your little princess sister can't use you to practice her diva skills."

Junie snorts as though she can read my mind.

"Oh, shit, I didn't bring cash. Kyle, can we have forty bucks? Abby and me will get you a present!" she says, her voice sounding all babyish.

He hands her two twenties.

Junie's tits seem to be exploding from her dumb Renaissance bodice. She's a fair maiden with rust-colored lip-goop.

Kyle's glasses show a tiny crack near the frame.

I want to stay with him, but I follow Junie into the crowd of jugglers, kings, queens, whores, and clowns.

As soon as she is distracted, I scoot away and buy a roast turkey leg. I sit on a cider barrel, savoring the meat, eating all the fatty parts—un-feminine and exhilarating. It tastes only a bit less perfect than I imagined.

From beneath a tree, I watch Junie flirt with a henchman selling large, silver pendants. She once told me she flirts to teach me how to do it, and part of this is true; I don't know how, or even want to. But really, she's just hoping he'll give her something free.

Kyle doesn't buy anything, and we don't even try to find a present for him either. That night, at Junie's house, I keep waking up, imagining the leather water bottle holder I might have bought him. He works at the pet store on weekends—I know this because I've seen him there when I'm with Mom buying dog supplies. Junie says Kyle has no friends and he has nothing better to do with his time on weekends.

"He takes lame-ass jobs," she says.

HUMAN NATURE

IT'S ABOUT FINDING YOURSELF inside the wispy days of knowing all you can stand to watch is *Animal Planet,* because animals are so much more interesting than humans.

For example, Mom thinks Daniel is a decent person. It all started when Mom sat next to him in a wellness class, where he stuck to her like a tick. At first he talked all about mindfulness and herbology—supportive of her fight with cancer. Now he just watches TV.

When Junie comes over, Daniel gets out of the TV chair. He tries out his raunchier jokes when Mom is out of earshot.

"Junie and Abby-bug: What is the difference between parsley and pussy?"

Neither of us answer.

Daniel sells health insurance and says he cracks his clients up.

Mom has stripped her throat so many times yelling at Daniel about how he drives down to the beach after he drinks a six-pack.

"He's going to kill someone soon," she says.

"I would not drive if I were truly intoxicated! Good freaking Lord," he says.

Every night now, he sleeps in the living room chair with the TV on.

FRECKLES

FRECKLES ON MY FACE, MY ARMS, MY BACK. Freckles on my lips, flecks of oil, or butter, or tomato sauce on my t-shirts. Everywhere I'm spotted, defective. Sometimes people's eyes follow my freckles, as if I'm a bruised banana. Junie has confidence. No freckles at all, and a long neck. Mostly, I'm envious of her low voice. She has the kind of voice you can impress people with. At sixteen, it sounds as if she's been smoking cigarettes for forty years.

She sleeps over and I feel myself grow quiet around bedtime; I can't come up with funny stories. I would like to ask her a few things about her brother, but know better.

She starts investigating my room for something to tease me about. When she crawls under my bed, I see her belly button popping out.

"Is this your widdle teddy bear, *Abby-bug?*" she asks.

She's holding Ted, my childhood pal, a ripped bear with a babyish face. I kept him in bed with me until a few years ago, a mortifying habit.

Holding Ted, giggling maniacally, Junie is trying to make him squeak like a dog toy. She's perfect and mean as a TV star.

I slide next to her under the bed, so she won't break Ted's

neck by forcing him to do things he can't. It's dumb, but I want to give Ted to my own kids someday.

I kiss her on the lips to save him.

TEPID

I HAVE MANY PROBLEMS TO GNAW ON. One of them is the way Daniel blathers at Mom when Mom is resting. He'll burst in to talk about the lame fact that "tepid" liquids are really the best temperature for the human body to digest. He says that if a person eats food at just the right temperature, it can fight the recurrence of cancer.

"Tepid everything!" he bellows at her as though it is so important she should stop resting.

"I'm lucky. Do you think it's easy to find someone when you're a middle-aged widow with cancer?" Mom barked at me when I ask her why she forgives Daniel.

Dad always knocked before he entered a room.

I take the napkin and wipe my lips, glance at Mom pouring Kona—her holiday splurge.

"Straight from Hawaii," she brags, winking—as if it were illegal.

Daniel puts his weight on our least stable chair, leaning it back. He wants to break his ass so we'll have to feel sorry for him, to wait on him.

The dots on Daniel's shirt are dumb; he looks like a cartoon salesman.

I pop my knuckles watching him sip Mom's Kona, *The Wall Street Journal* next to him for comfort.

"Paper's soggy again."

I narrow my eyes and make ugly, cartoonish expressions at him so he doesn't look too hard at Mom.

Daniel puts his foot on mine and smiles. "Leave this old man alone, Abby-bug," he says. He is the one who should leave me alone. And he does, because I am smarter than him, and I usually see what's coming next.

I'm wearing Mom's enormous hoop earrings because they make me feel like I can kick his ass.

"Coffee for either of you?" Mom says.

"I'm good," I say, glancing at her quickly.

She looks down at her shoes with a soft grin. She's been spiking Daniel's coffee with her anti-depressants for a few weeks, sure they will balance his moods. Problem is, they aren't "moods" and she can't make him likable. It is just who he is.

MORRO BAY

DANIEL'S USED FOREIGN CAR BREAKS DOWN right there at Avila Beach, near Morro Bay. He says the guts of the car are cheap. He says for the hundredth time that nothing surprises him.

He'll soon be my step-dad, Mom says, and tells me in a serious voice that it is kinder to be pleasant.

It's Saturday and he is taking me on a field trip up around Morro Bay so I can see exactly where he grew up. This seems to mean a lot to him and he's wearing extra-stinky air-freshener cologne.

"Up here near Morro Bay, the ocean looks indigo," I say.

Indigo is my favorite color, and I may be just wishing the water to be this color. Or else, it is just something to say.

The California coastline is being ruined by oil derricks, but the lights on them are festive-looking, like a sea party.

You can see the bluest part of the ocean from the highway up near Diablo Nuclear Power Plant.

We're stopped along the shoulder. I remember the first night with the new used car, when he proudly took the whole top off by touching a button.

"Why did I buy a fucking convertible, Abby?" he asks. "Why am I so fucking stupid?"

As if I know. He seems to imagine a lever that can reset things by asking.

And he believes that because I am a teenager he can swear in front of me.

"Freeway air is bad shit, so breathe through your nose."

I pretend to do that, tightening my lips hard. In the passenger seat mirror, I try and make my nostrils flare.

Mom's hair is dry as Astroturf these days. Aunt Susan sent me an e-mail telling me to keep my eye on her. The e-mail said, "She may need many injections of vitamin D if she's not getting outdoors, just tell her boyfriend to get her to a nutritionist."

She tells me, as always, that I have not missed anything, including the hot miserable summer in Pittsburgh. She says in her e-mail, like she always does, that I am a lucky girl. "Thank God our summer is over," she says.

I write back and tell her that every summer I miss seeing lightning bugs.

Daniel says AAA will be here soon, and we should just listen to the sound of the ocean for a while.

"Hey, you smell like flowers," he says. He must mean my shampoo, but it is not any different. I look out my window and try to find something to lock eyes on. There are a few ugly buildings and I stare hard at a parking lot. I can feel his eyes on my neck and chest. Men are like this, but Daniel has X-ray eyes. I feel like he can see my bones.

"You and your ma. You're my girls," he says.

He takes my hand, places it firmly in his jacket pocket,

then moves the pocket with our hands held together directly over his jeans to the place where it's all swollen up and animal-like. I feel my stomach twist. He holds my hand there and asks me to describe what I am feeling.

"Tell me why it's warm here," he says.

His breath poisons the air. This is the first time I feel afraid of Daniel, but it's too late—he's done something that will stick to my brain.

I want to wrench my arm away and smack his puffy face, but I don't because he is the driver of the car, and all I want is to get home. He holds my hand tightly.

"Quiet, aren't we?" he says.

MOLD

MY LEGS AND BACK ITCH, my hair is frizzy, and I have gotten skinnier because I hate eating at the table and hearing Daniel swallow food.

When his eyes, like fruit flies, land on my tits—I pretend I can swat them off. I never look right into them. Instead, I stare hard at the bullseye on the bridge of his nose.

Our windows weep and colors form in splotches on the walls. A gray-green mold line is framing our baseboards. Unless someone sprays mold with bleach, it will behave just like it wants to. You can't stop mold from being itself.

If the house sinks into the ground it will feel right at home. The house and the ground seem to be finding each other.

UNDERGROUND

I THINK ALL MOM REALLY WANTS is for someone decent to slice cucumbers for her swollen eyes in the morning. Summer is over and the days are growing short, so there's no time to get everything done, she says. I don't know what "everything" is, because she isn't really working. She feels ugly I guess, and that is why she doesn't like to leave the house much. Crying is normal, so who cares if her eyelids are purple?

Daniel hates it when people or dogs look sad. I don't understand why he doesn't re-plaster some of the holes in our walls, or do a bit of painting. Why he doesn't accompany Mom for walks.

When I was little, I searched for salamanders and worms in our backyard after the rains. When I found them, I picked them up with my fingers and took them to the cleaner part of the yard. What I didn't know then is that I was killing them by exposing their wormy asses to predatory birds.

Maybe I want to live underground and only squirm out occasionally. Mainly, I'd like to stop worrying about Mom and the way asymmetrical stains have taken over our ceiling.

Maybe I wish Junie's brother Kyle were not Junie's brother, because he seems as though he'd listen and not make fun of me for the way I think.

Sometimes I pass by The Animal Place on weekends, when he's working, and wave.

Mom listens to National Public Radio a lot and tells me that our Earth is losing this long, shitty marriage with humans.

"Planet Earth, we really had a swell time ruining you!" she says.

"Thanks for, you know... giving birth to me," I say.

There are very good men in the world, but like earthworms, they are not easily visible.

Mom insists on neighborhood clean-up, makes me go with her to the little park and pick up candy wrappers and condoms and cans and dog shit. I wash my hands again and again.

CRISP

MOM LOVES BEAN WITH BACON SOUP; the hickory smell reminds her of camping, she says. She tells me how my Dad was good-looking in a crisp way. She says I am crisp too, that I resemble him.

"What the fuck does that mean?" I say. I have no idea what looking *crisp* means. I'm not being rude.

She pops my face, then she says, "You may be a rocket scientist someday, honey, but you will never be kind."

She has no breasts so there is no way to be mad at her now.

There is a wheeze and puff inside her voice that seems permanent since her surgery. For some reason, when she talks about Dad these days, it makes me angry.

She loves the fall, and it has always been our favorite season—but everything she likes seems to have changed recently, and there is no knowing what she will like these days.

DOUBLE DATE

WE'VE EATEN TWO POT BROWNIES APIECE, and Junie is impressed that we are picked up in a four-door BMW. It belongs to one of the boy's parents. The car smells like honey and cat food.

The less-cute one has Jesus-like hair and a canvas shirt. The other boy is exotic looking, with dark skin and light eyes.

When the long-haired boy sees me there in the back seat, I say, "Let there be light." He doesn't get the joke.

I take what he gives me from his hands, hoping they are clean.

I can't imagine they are sterile, so no way do I want to ingest it. I put the mushroom in my mouth and hold it there inside my cheek while making a gulping sound, coughing loudly so he'll turn his head away.

"Blessings," he says, already high and stupid.

"My dog is on my shoulder," he says. "His name is Bailboy."

I guess he tells me this right off, so he can show me a tattoo of the dog face on his shoulder—but really so I can see his muscles.

"I've earned a dog like this," he says.

"Prison Guard is a funny dog name, too," I say.

I am not funny to him, or to myself.

He asks me if I have ever done mushrooms before this. He says he likes what he sees on my face.

We are laughing, or else dogs are barking so loud from somewhere they are stripping their throats. Soon, his lips surround mine, his tongue pushing in and swimming around inside my mouth.

Outside the car, I see a row of brownish pines. Junie is making out with the Brazilian kid.

While the boy is kissing me, home is what I keep thinking about—how I will pass out from the brownies I've eaten but Mom loves me and will argue my case if we're busted.

The boy's weird hair pulls on my earring, and I push him away to fix it.

My head's skipping around the world—everything feels remote and unusual, like a foreign movie.

"Wanna swap?"

Junie spits these words into the car window. They play in my mind for a minute.

"Swap?" I can't tell if that is what she had said, so I ask the boy if she said that.

"Yep."

Spinning in circles next to the car, like a bottle or a toddler, extending her arm and index finger, Junie points at all of us—but stops on me.

"You!" she says.

Junie is smarter than I thought.

My body is done with this, and my legs begin running toward the road.

STEMS

I WEAR SUNGLASSES INDOORS THESE DAYS, trying not to seem disgusted with the way the floor creaks everywhere I step. It is impossible to be quiet in this house, because nothing is sturdy.

I avoid Daniel whenever possible. Mom wears a plain gold band on her ring finger now. I try not to look at it, but when I see it I can't help but worry about her brain—how she's gotten so weak she's planning to marry such a pitiful person. Even worse—she doesn't give a rat's ass what I think, or she'd ask. I bite my fingernails down to mushroom stems.

Junie's brother Kyle is someone I want to know better since he does not care about being cool or even normal because he never will be. I like the idea of being the kind of person who doesn't care about what people think.

At school, I like my writing and psychology classes. They're the only subjects I pay attention in. I wish they'd stop forcing people to do the stuff they don't like, which for me is all the rest.

During lunch, I eat with Junie up at the Burger Place. These days her skinny makeup-obsessed friends come along. When I slip out and leave, nobody notices, so I sit in the library and read about animal adaptations or rare diseases.

Kyle hides behind his glasses, as I am learning to.

SINGING

MOM IS SINGING, WITH HER OLD BREASTS, in my dream. Daniel hates her singing voice, but she is singing anyway.

She never wants to say the words *we are stuck,* so she sings them instead.

But then it is clear it is a dream, because this is not Daniel, it is Dad. I can smell the beer on his breath, which Mom used to hate. He is nervous and foot-tapping, which was what he did when he didn't want to talk about stuff. It is really him.

He says the holes in my shoes and the inky scribblings on them ruin my looks. He says they are not cool looking, just broken. Then he says that the holes will somehow get smaller.

In the dream, we are laughing, but I can't figure out what we're laughing about.

FIELDS OF CHEESE

I'M AT FIELDS OF CHEESE, A PIZZA PLACE, in the older, less popular mall downtown, when I notice Kyle in line a bit ahead of me.

We both say *hey* but don't look at one another directly. Kyle makes me jumpy. I wish one of us were not shy. Two shy people sort of cancel each other out.

He is ordering The Goatherd. "Everything but onions."

He then explains to me that he's allergic to onions: white, purple, red, and pearl.

I'm looking down at my shoes, which I've written on and cut uneven holes in. He glances at them, and mumbles something about how much he likes them.

"I ruined them, but thanks," I say.

"Better ugly," he says.

All I can think about is what I heard on the news recently—a report about disease brought on by drought. Like invisible monsters, these disease atoms seize you and kill you while you are doing something like choosing a pizza, trying to relax.

Maybe you never liked choosing a pizza combination anyway, maybe you wish somebody would do it for you, but you don't deserve to die yet.

I ask him about the birds at the Bird Refuge. He says he visits them mostly because one of the ducks there used to belong to his family. Their dog bit off her tail feathers, so she's easy to spot.

"She was halfway in his mouth when I rescued her," he says. Junie had not told me about any of this. She just says Kyle's weird. I wonder what she says about me when I'm not there. It is freeing to be here with her brother and to be able to feel as weird as I want.

He has no idea how much is wrong with my life.

Someone skinny and odd like Kyle needs something to lean on, so I smile at him as much as my mouth will do so.

New age magazine ads say that if we buy and wear their expensive sex hormone oil, we'll heal and live like animals again. Our brains are depressed and taking too many meds just trying to hack back home, into our spirits.

Over at his table, Kyle smiles behind his sunglasses—and soon I'm telling him that I like ducks and herons, which is more or less true. I would like to go with him to the Bird Refuge sometime, I say.

HELIUM

CARBONATED CAT IS MY FAVORITE DRINK. It's my sixteenth birthday. This was what Mom and Dad always concocted for my birthdays, this kiddie cocktail. Mom mixes spicy ginger ale with Grenadine, and then adds plenty of Tequila to Daniel's drink. She's still not allowed to drink coffee or booze. At her last check up, she was clean of cancer.

We sit out on the fraying porch watching baby spiders bubble out from the ancient wood floor. Mom says we should all toast to me. Daniel says there is nothing to toast to. Mom is very still.

Daniel says, "Let's toast to the great idea that this young lady may become something some day."

There are sharp, coughing noises from a motorcycle down the block, and further, down the block, the old guy screaming at his dog a million times.

I throw my glass and it crashes into the weeds. Mom and I are standing and I tell her in a loud voice what he is—what he did to me in his car.

I don't know why it is not embarrassing anymore. I want to paint it all over the ruined house.

He says I am full of hateful lies and what a spoiled little tale-spinner I have become.

Mom is taller than I have ever seen her.

"This child has never lied to me. Now, get the fuck out!!"
Daniel's face is red and he looks like a fat, old man. He
can't do much about it since I am calling the police and he
knows the neighbors are listening. We live all squashed
together here, houses on houses. Our yards are tiny. If you
took all of the fences down, our backyards would blend
into a dog park.

Daniel goes inside to pack up and we sit there tightly
holding hands, Mom and I, like helium balloons trying to
stay down here on Earth.

DUCKS

SATURDAY, IN THE LATE AFTERNOON, Kyle and I are at the Bird Refuge, watching ducks and geese shuffle around and squawk in unison, like band warmup.

Kyle tells me that last summer he worked at the zoo, at the zoo-mobile rides. I loved those as a kid, I tell him.

Then we start talking all over the place about zoo animals and idiotic parents and their smart-ass kids and we talk on this subject for a surprisingly long time. I'm getting cold, and it's late. The sun is drooping way down toward the ocean.

I slip off my shoes and massage my toes, while he watches me rub them. They hurt when I'm angry and upset.

"Don't go barefoot here, you can get an infection that will eat your flesh from bird shit," Kyle says.

He sounds like a guy who is good at knowing about rare diseases, which is something I would like to get good at too. Kyle wears hiking boots.

I put my shoes back on, buckle them, say, "That's what I need, my flesh eaten."

The duck nearest to us has only a few tail feathers, looks obscene and naked compared with the rest, and basically stays clear of other ducks. It is his duck, of course. It squawks more than the rest.

"Do you smoke stuff?" he asks.

I tell him that I am not smoking anything. This is mostly true. I am not smoking anything addictive, and I only do it on weekends when I can get some from Junie, which isn't that often.

He shakes his head and smiles.

Suddenly, I wonder when he started coming out here alone, visiting the ducks. Probably, like any odd person, he is able to do what he likes because he's already been labeled by people. Maybe nothing matters to him about that kind of stuff anymore.

"You are pretty," he says.

I feel blood in my face, my cheeks.

He clears his throat, and says he'd like me to meet him again tomorrow.

A feeling of worry overtakes me, working its way to my cheeks.

"I'll try," I say, walking away, skating through piles of bird waste.

WINTER

THE WEATHER CHANNEL'S TALKING HEADS, all Botoxed and baby-fatted in their cheeks, ramble on about radical snowstorms in Pennsylvania. When we first moved here, I wanted to paint the leaves around our house white.

Driving downtown, I count the fake blondes wearing sexy winter gear and two-dollar Santa hats. It's always warm enough here to wear shorts.

Mom is getting outside again, and her face has freckles.

Daniel is gone and the house is ours. The foundation is still cracking, but the inside smells better.

Bruno and I take long walks and I think about why I haven't gone back to meet Kyle. He has told me not to worry about it. He says when I'm ready, he'll be there. Says the right things.

Sweat trickles down my back. Bruno pants. I promise him that someday we'll skate on firm ice alongside our own man.

NATURE

I READ ABOUT HOW FLATFISH live on the bottom of the ocean floor. How they are born with one eye on each side of their heads, which is not useful because they are flat. How, eventually, one of their eyes begins to move until both eyes are on the same side of their head, and they can see in all directions. That is an example of just how smart nature is.

Say your mom lived with a salesman con-artist—someone who treated the world as his trash can, because she had her eyes closed. You could understand some of this, but you couldn't see it all, because you were too afraid to move. Because your eyes were not helping each other.

I like to believe that being without Daniel has made Mom better. But these days she watches so much television that she glows with blue light.

ILLUSIONS

SOMETIMES KYLE AND I MAKE FACES to crack each other up. Sometimes I laugh so hard I nearly choke, the laughing takes over like hiccoughs.

"Can you die swallowing your own spit?" I ask.

We talk about having an evening picnic. I'll bring my silly Optical Illusion book and he'll bring a flashlight. We do kid-like stuff and we like it this way.

Sometimes I worry that we'll burn out if we spend too much time together, but we have been seeing each other every weekend this summer.

The illusions have names like the Cornsweet illusion, the Hollow-Face illusion, and the Chubb illusion. I wonder about the freaks who invented them.

Laying on a blanket in my front yard with the book and flashlight, he says: "Sometimes I forget that you're my sister's friend."

"Junie's so freaked out by us she hangs with anyone who'll pay her way," I say.

He pets my hair and I close my eyes. My shirt is light and loose, because it's hot out.

He asks if he can touch me up inside my blouse.

"Your hands are just soft enough," I say.

Under my shirt, his fingers trace my sports bra. He covers my right breast and it warms.

I wonder what he is feeling there. I never imagine there is cancer growing inside my body when Kyle is around.

While he holds me, I stare straight up at the almost-round smile of moon. The sky is so clear that stars pop out like lightning bugs.

"You," he says. "Sit in here."

He opens his legs, and I sit up against him like a wall.

He says he lives in dreams but he wants that to end. This feels like a scene in a movie that comes somewhere right near the middle, when the popcorn tastes just right.

ABOUT THE AUTHOR

MEG POKRASS is the author of *Damn Sure Right* (Press 53, 2011) and *Bird Envy* (Printed on Paige, 2014). Her flash fiction appears in 200 literary journals including *Green Mountains Review, Five Points, storySouth, McSweeney's,* and *Flash Fiction International* (W.W. Norton, 2015). Meg is currently co-writing humor with Bobbie Ann Mason and was recently commissioned to write an original film with veteran screenwriter Graham Gordy. Meg serves as associate editor for Rick Barthelme's *New World Writing*. She lives in San Francisco with a dog and two cats. Find out more at megpokrass.com.

3 | AARON TEEL

A Brief Crack of Light:
Mimicking Memory in the Novella-in-Flash

Shampoo Horns

A BRIEF CRACK OF LIGHT:
MIMICKING MEMORY IN THE NOVELLA-IN-FLASH

> "The cradle rocks above an abyss, and common sense
> tells us that our existence is but a brief crack of light
> between two eternities of darkness."
>
> —VLADIMIR NABOKOV,
> *SPEAK, MEMORY*

AS A FORM, THE NOVELLA-IN-FLASH closely approximates
my own experience, moving as it does from one anxious,
fleeting moment to the next. When a succession of
moments has receded far enough away, the memories
that remain are mixed up and weird, disconnected, out of
time—they come to me in flashes.

To the extent that memory is the hidden conceit in
Shampoo Horns, the novella-in-flash is its ideal form. Its
arc is made of moments rather than a single, novelistic
through-line—fumbling desires accessed by a consciousness
reaching back through the static for stories that stick firmly
and unaccountably in the mind like bits of broom-straw
driven through a telephone pole by the force of tornado. I
have never seen my own consciousness reflected in the long
arc of a novel.

Flash, as a form, is surprisingly malleable. There are
as many ways to approach it as writers who write it—

which is to say, there are a lot. But the flashes that stick are real stories that surprise with language and sharply rendered imagery, revealing some hidden or unarticulated experience in an unexpected flash of light. Every word in so small a space has to be weighed and measured. Every sentence has to earn its keep. The novella-in-flash allows for what is good about this constraint—the tension that grows in the distance between narrative concision and linguistic invention—and marries it to what is good about longer forms. There is space for striving and change and emotional investment in the people on the page. If flash fetishizes the moment, the novella-in-flash provides a space for myriad moments to co-exist, rub up against, and reverberate off of one another. If flash is allergic to exposition and summary—if it revels in language and detail and scene—then the novella-in-flash allows the details to accumulate and the images to grow and twist and repeat. If a single flash is a snapshot then the novella-in-flash is a slideshow projected onto a bed-sheet scavenged from the hamper and pinned to the wall above the television set. Or a book of overlapping Polaroids held haphazardly in place by static electricity and thin plastic sheets.

Each story in a novella-in-flash should be self-contained and fully fleshed enough to stand alone and end with no gimmicks or worthless, easy twists, while simultaneously being able to function within a larger narrative frame, however fractured, abstracted, or oblique. In shaping *Shampoo Horns*, I cut stories that fit within the frame but weren't strong enough to carry their own weight or leaned too heavily on the others, as well as stories that worked and were self-contained but didn't in any way add to or deepen the larger narrative arc. The flashes that made the cut don't compress time so much as fully inhabit individual moments, treating each as entities unto themselves rather than part of some smooth and continuous chain. Moments are magnified and the transitions cut away so that the stories are distinct but inextricably linked. What might seem superfluous in a novel—small enough to be glossed over or pushed aside for the sake of the singular narrative line—is here allowed to take center stage. A surreptitiously snapped photo of a boy half turned away, a tack stuck in one of the rough-skinned soles of his perpetually bare feet, two girls spinning in skates around bewildered brothers standing on skateboards on a darkening, lamp-lit street— the reader is allowed to observe and dwell in each moment as it comes rather than rushing forward for some grand, angels-singing sort of climax. The novella-in-flash allows for climaxes on top of climaxes all along the way.

Memories are finicky and not easily aligned. They're framed by eras marked by tragedy or triumph or change. Cherry Tree's memories come to him in pieces that he places in time before or after a tornado—the temporal frame in which these stories spin. The links between the first and penultimate piece are sometimes associative rather than chronological or causal. His attempts to organize his mind don't always succeed. Memory is not easily summoned by force of will; smells and tastes and the totemic power of objects are often required. Experience is anchored to physicality, to particular textures and colors and shapes. Plastic cups, switchblade combs, pink flamingos with missing heads, tight red underwear, and tattered towels worn as capes—these are the concrete tokens of a specific time and place.

Denis Johnson's *Jesus' Son* was one of the models for *Shampoo Horns'* fragmented form—offering the twin revelations that such small spaces could be stuffed with so much music, incantatory language, and teeming, desirous life and that a book could be a space for a character to dwell and roam around in rather than move through in an unbroken line. Sherwood Anderson's *Winesburg, Ohio* was another, with its lovingly rendered dirt, detail, and poetry of the moment, the everyday. The short works of Lydia Davis, Diane Williams, Donald Barthelme, and countless others expanded my notions of what and how much could be done in the space of a page, and Vladimir Nabokov's sense-driven, episodic memoir *Speak, Memory* was the unreachable ideal I reached for. I had designs to write my own kind of fractured Nabokovian memoir of encroaching adolescence set in a sun-struck trailer park rather than a comfortable aristocratic house in the Russian countryside. But while I mined my own memory for images and inspiration, these are ultimately fictions rendered with a form and language meant to mimic the act of remembering.

Reconstructing memory into coherent narrative is one

way of ascribing meaning to all these endlessly receding moments. What else is fiction for? What else art? *Shampoo Horns* is one kind of story, or set of stories, or both, that the novella-in-flash is suited to, an approximation of this kind of experience: one anxious, fleeting moment at a time.

—AARON TEEL

SHAMPOO HORNS

BY AARON TEEL

TABLE OF CONTENTS

SHAMPOO HORNS

"THE DEVIL'S BRAND IS ON YOUR BONES," Dad says, pausing by the bathroom door with a bottle of Shiner and a rolled-up newspaper.

"Don't you listen to that," my mother whispers, and pours a red plastic cup full of bathwater over my head. "You've been washed in the blood of the Lamb."

Two brown girls in too-big t-shirts and white roller skates with white laces spin in circles around me every night in the street outside our trailer, and I stole one of my mother's rings to give to Lupe, the younger one, because I love her and I thought she would like it. My mother and Jesus have thoroughly forgiven me.

"My little Casanova," she says, and I feel her nails on my scalp, her breath on my neck. I smell the cafeteria grease that lingers on her clothes and hair and skin. The blood in the water is from a cut I took from a steel burr on a chain-link fence I leaped over, running home, after Lupe told me her mother gave the ring back to mine because it was too nice. Outside there are broken televisions and busted toilets, pink flamingos with missing heads.

My best friend Tater Tot lives two trailers down with his mother who is drunk all the time, and sad. Tater's small for his age, has a terrible lisp, and wears a blonde chili-bowl haircut that bounces up and down when he runs. My half-brother Clay is sixteen. He's rebellious and mean and I know I will never be as cool as him. Gas Pedal is a game we play where he holds my ankles and crushes my balls with his feet. Our dad, perpetually sunburned with his sports page and beer, mutters "dad-gums," "gall-dangs" and "dag-nabbits" at no one in particular. Tina is the sexy teenage babysitter in tight stonewashed jean shorts and neon green halter-tops who made me ramen-wiener stew, got herself knocked up and had to quit school, and I know no other woman will ever compare. Shep Milton owns the park and lives in the biggest trailer, a double-wide painted pink with bright white security lights attached that come on if you get too close. A family of animals cut from stone makes its home in his yard, placed there and cared for by Mrs. Milton, who always wears a nightgown and never goes anywhere further than the juniper bushes that mark the edge of their lot. Shep wears jogging pants that whistle when he walks and his belly is big but hard as a rock. He runs a fireworks stand in the summer and sometimes secretly sleeps with Tater's mother. Buster is the stray husky Dad feeds from his own plate and lets lick the salt from his sun-blistered face. I'm the twelve-year-old boy sitting naked in the bath, happy to have his mother washing his heaps of curly red hair, twisting it into shampoo horns and laughing.

We lived for many years in a rented trailer in Galveston, facing the sea, but Dad saved enough through hard work and sweat to buy this ready-made trailer and park it on a densely treed lot in a mobile home park in Seaview, Texas, a place nowhere near the sea that smells always of slaughtered cattle and manure and rendered fat from the meatpacking and processing plant that sits just upwind and blots out the sun with great white plumes of smoke. "The cloud factory," Dad sometimes calls it, but I know better. Seaview exists mainly in the peripheral vision or rearview mirrors of folks passing through on their way to Corpus Christi or Padre Island or someplace altogether better.

HOLES

IF GOD OR THE ANGELS were to have looked down at the A-1 mobile home park in the months before it was rearranged by a mid-summer tornado, He or they would have seen through the smoke the flat rectangle tops of thirteen trailers lined up in two crooked rows alongside a thick tangle of oak trees. He or they would have seen a hot-looking place, low to the ground, with thirteen dented roofs like old tin cans lined up and shot through with BB guns, and He or they would have seen me walking around it barefoot in a uniform of faded Superman Underoos, with a tattered towel tied around my neck.

I never wore shoes or pants in the summer unless forced by my mother for church or the grocery store, so the soles of my feet were tough as leather and tar-black. I once stepped on a tack that stayed stuck in my foot for days or maybe as long as a week before I pulled it out, quick-as-you-please, careless as a nail from a tire. The bottom of the tack was black to match the soles of my feet and scraped smooth from the road. I'd heard it down there for some time, scratching and clicking, but hadn't bothered to look. There was a bloodless hole in my sole when I pulled it out. Later I missed the tack's clickety-clack company and found another of equal size and shape pinning a glossy 8x10 of Kerry Von Erich to my bedroom wall. It fig snugly into the hole left by its twin.

Tater Tot, my one and only friend, blew by me on his bike and squeezed its horrible horn, a sound like a braying donkey swallowing a kazoo. He skidded to a stop and pushed himself backward with his feet to where I stood.

"Hey Cherry," he said. "You wanna go up to the Food Lion and look at comicth?" (I was called Cherry Tree then, or Cherry, or Tree, or CT, but never Matthew or Matty or Matt—not even by my mother—because I was tall for my age and thin as a rail, she said, and my hair was a mess of bright red curls, only tangentially a part of my head, that refused to be corralled or put into place.)

"Can't," I said. "Clay's comin' tomorrow. I gotta clean my room."

"Thath your brother," Tater said. It wasn't a question; it was a recitation of learned fact. He was looking down at his own feet when he said it. They were clad in disintegrating flip-flops, but no less dirty than mine. Tater was eleven years old, a grade below me in school, but he looked far younger, like an overgrown toddler without a shirt, shielding his eyes from the sun and balancing on tippy toes to keep his bike from falling. The floppy fringe of his sun-bleached bowl cut lay atop his fingers and reminded me of the thatched roof that covered a grass hut I saw in *National Geographic* while looking for pictures of breasts, and I thought of the woman who stood in front of it, her skin so black it fairly glowed, and the way the infant on her hip seemed to grow from her body like a tumor or a tiny twin.

"He has to come early," I said, "on account-a he got into some trouble."

Tater shook his head knowingly and looked around. "I counted that Methican girl'th holeth lath night," he said, motioning with a nod toward the trailer where we'd watched her move in with her older sister and what we took to be their mother and father, but Tater told me later was really their mother and uncle. "Illegalth," he added, with the conspiratorial tone of a man revealing the true nature of things.

We'd been sitting in the street reading comics in the fading light when their old Chevy truck, several shades of red and brown with a trash bag flapping where the rear window should have been, came around the corner and sputtered to a stop in front of Mr. Healer's old trailer. Mr. Healer had died from a heart attack two weeks after being laid off from the plant and was carried out shirtless on a gurney in the predawn hours, according to Dad, who'd been on his way out the door when the ambulance arrived.

"He cleaned out the blood tanks," Mom said. "Inhaled too much a-that chlorine and it burnt him up from the inside out." Mom worked in the cafeteria at the plant, but Tater's mother, when sloshed on vodka, confided in her the gory details of the factory floor, and she dutifully confided them to me.

The girls emerged from the depths of the truck's cabin,

following their mother, who was small and round, and a man in a greasy ball cap and thick black mustache. They looked like twins at first, with their oval faces and skin the color of the raw almonds offered to us from a glass bowl at one of the houses in the development where Tater's mother took us trick-or-treating on Halloween, hoping for better candy, but one was taller and older than the other. They spotted us watching them and giggled. For the first time in my life I felt embarrassed sitting nearly naked in the street, wearing a ragged towel for a cape. We watched them carry in a few bags of clothes and food and an exotic looking rug embroidered with a colorful image of Christ and the Virgin Mary.

"She wath pretty good at it," he added, with all seriousness and generosity.

Neither of us had ever really counted anybody's holes, but we lied about it freely to one another with creative abandon. I knew enough at least to know by which hole God rendered copies of Himself, but Tater probably didn't. He wasn't fully retarded, but his mother was a drunk raising him alone and he had no brother to show him the way.

BOONDOCKS

CLAY SET A GIRL'S HAIR ON FIRE. That's why his mother sent him to live with us. She'd had enough, she said, and Dad paced back and forth around the phone mounted above the dinner table, getting tangled up in its plastic web.

It was the first week of June when Clay arrived with a duffel bag full of clothes and a check for two hundred dollars that Dad tore into little pieces and threw in my yellow Pac-Man trash can. "I don't know who she thinks she is," he said, and stalked out of our room, grumbling.

He was bored and she was wearing too much hairspray. That's why he said he did it. She had second-degree burns on her neck and scalp and the judge threatened him with juvenile detention. I wore pants and shoes to the airport and left my towel at home, but I wore the rest of my uniform beneath. My mother stood behind me with one hand on my shoulder and her hair pulled back in its unrelenting bun. "Welcome Clay-y," she said, "we've been a-waitin'."

Dad's Ranger, bought used from a lot in Corpus Christi, was washed and shined for the occasion as he was manly proud of it, but Clay didn't say "nice truck" or "when did you get this" or make any kind of comment at all. He rode all the way home in the back, clutching his skateboard, with his dirty blonde curls whipping in the wind, and Dad said the Devil's brand was on his bones.

My mother helped him put away his things and spoke loudly about nothing. She made a casserole and we ate it around our too-small kitchen table with our elbows and knees touching and our plates threatening to fall. After dinner we watched the news and Clay went outside three times to smoke. Every time he went out Mom looked at me with her eyebrows and mouth all scrunched up together and shook her head, solemn as a monk. She said, "Don't you let him make you smoke, I can't believe his mother lets him do that, if I catch you doing any of that," and so on in that way, until he'd come back in and she would cut off mid-sentence and pretend to be engrossed in a report on a local school board controversy or the rising cost of lemons.

"That'll be your last pack," Dad said, "You'd best make it last."

Later on, Clay opened our bedroom window and crawled out into the bosom of the oak that stood just outside, and from there onto the trailer's roof. "You want to have a smoke?" he asked, and I climbed out after him and sat on the edge of the overhanging roof, bravely letting my legs dangle. He handed me a Lucky and struck a match in front of my face. When I tried to stick the end of the cigarette in the flame he laughed, not unkindly, and said, "You have to put it in your mouth first."

"Oh yeah," I said, "I forgot." I put the Lucky between my lips and Clay lit the tip and I inhaled deep to show my toughness, then broke into a fit of wild coughing. He laughed again and patted me on the back.

"You'd better not let your mom catch you smoking. She'd shit." I took another drag and held it in my cheeks. "I can't believe how fucked this place is," he said, shaking his head at the billowing smokestack. "What a fucking stink."

"You forget about it after a while, though," I said. He took another puff from his own cigarette and exhaled the words, "This is the for real fucking boondocks."

"What's boondocks?" I asked, and he said, "This, man. This is fucking boondocks," and he made a gesture with his hand that damned the whole world as boondocks, and the moon and all the stars as well. He stood up and crushed his butt beneath the heel of a battered Chuck Taylor and leaped straight off the roof and back into the arms of the oak. "I'm going for a walk," he said, and started to shimmy down it. "Don't tell them I left or anything, ok?"

"Ok," I said, and watched him walk out of the park and be swallowed up by the darkness and the trees, both of which I was deathly afraid and, at any rate, were forbidden to me by my mother.

THE BABYSITTER'S TRAILER

TINA WAS MY BABYSITTER for one and one-quarter summers, but the changes she wrought were irrevocable. I learned the meaning of the dirty balls of her feet when she fell asleep on her mother's couch, stretched out like a dog, and how when her toes curled and popped it meant she'd wake up soon, make us bologna sandwiches or ramen noodles with chopped up wieners and give us peppermint candies from the bottom of her purse for dessert. In the babysitter's trailer there was Madonna and MTV; there was homemade vanilla ice cream. In the babysitter's trailer there was never any angry Jesus or Gas Pedals and there was always Tina, with her bleached blonde hair, crimping iron, and purple toe polish.

During the day, when school was out, Tina's trailer was the only one besides Shep's where anybody was home. She'd quit high school to babysit full time. She'd got herself knocked up, Clay said, but it was a while before I cottoned on to the idea that she was pregnant. At first she looked every bit the sweet and tender teenage queen she'd been the summer before, but by late May she had a pooch that she covered with a pillow when she lay on the couch, eating ice cream and watching her daytime stories.

She wore a purple bikini and lay out on a rainbow-colored folding chair that creaked when she moved. She kept the water hose on beside her and sprayed us with it if we stood in her sun.

"You jackals," she'd shout. "Quit yer crowdin' me," and Tater would run in circles around her chair until she sprayed him again.

Tina's mother caught me with my hands cupped to the glass of Tina's bedroom window, trying to see her change out of her bathing suit. "Dirty little shit," she said, and dragged me away by the ear. Mom wanted Dad to spank me but he wouldn't. "I can't blame the boy for lookin'," he said, and laughed.

TATER'S NIPPLE

"YOU'RE OLD ENOUGH to stay home with Clay," Dad declared over bowls of SpaghettiOs done his way, with two sandwich singles melting on top, "We'll save fifty smackers a week!" Mom grumbled quietly but couldn't argue when Dad spoke of smackers.

The months that followed are marked in my mind by the sight of the tornado that lifted Lupe's trailer from its lot and threw it headlong into a gully, the cuts and bruises acquired from being tied up in bedsheets, hung upside down from a tree limb and beaten about the chest and back with sticks, the dull ache that lingered after my crotch was used as a make-believe gas pedal for the Indy 500, and the taste left by fistfuls of grass that Clay shoved down my throat while he sat leering above me with his knees on my chest, his face a demonic silhouette fading in and out of shadow, the sun a blinding halo around his head that lit up his golden curls and made them burn.

At first Clay slept with me in the tiny bed handmade by our father before I was born, him fidgeting and rolling and stinking of cigarettes, me stone still, flat against the wall, barely breathing, but after a week Dad bought us an old set of bunk beds at yard sale. We made a fort out of them with sheets draped all the way around, and sat inside pretending to be Jedi Knights holed up and waiting for Storm Troopers to attack.

The wood panel walls in the hallway were narrow enough that we could put our feet on one wall and our hands on the other, then climb to the ceiling and hang suspended, pretending to be Spider-Man until our arms trembled and sent us falling face first into the stained linoleum. The biggest air conditioning vent was on the floor in the kitchen and when it kicked on we sat over it and pulled a white sheet over our heads that billowed up and made an ice-cold bubble around us that we imagined to be an igloo, and we spoke the way we imagined Eskimos would speak.

Clay went with me to Tater's trailer once, for a kick, to see what it was like. All the curtains were open but it seemed dark anyway. There were flies everywhere, and the sickly sweet smell of rotting meat. Plates of half-eaten food were scattered around the room amid piles of dirty laundry, stacks of comic books, decapitated action figures, and videotapes. The carpet was the color of sun-baked dog shit and a dead Christmas tree sagged in the corner of the room. I'd been there a million times and had stopped noticing, but seeing it through Clay's eyes, the way it really was, I was embarrassed and wanted to leave. "Let's get outta here," I said, but when we tried to leave Tater planted himself in front of the door and stomped and cried and begged us to stay. Clay reared back and kicked him in the balls, and he collapsed on the floor in a heap.

On the day I cut Tater's nipple off, five days after the tornado and three days after the 4th of July, the TV was on and he knocked on our screen door wearing only a pair of cutoff jean shorts so painfully too small for him that the zipper bulged vulgarly open and the fabric around the metal button was frayed to the point of snapping. It was early afternoon. We were watching cartoons and eating our daily ration of beef ravioli with chocolate milk. I was wearing dirty Superman Underoos, soaking wet from the tub. Tater stood in the doorway picking the caked dirt from beneath his fingernails with a set of metal clippers. I pushed open the door and asked what he wanted.

"Just theein' what you guys are doin' ith all," he said. "Theein' if you wanna come out and play or thumpin'." Behind him the street was littered with tree limbs, lawn decorations, bits of garbage and debris.

"Go home, Tater," Clay said.

"Well, d'ya think I can watch TV with you guyth? My mom'th home thick, watchin' her thtorieth."

Clay looked at me and shook his head. His thick eyebrows were scrunched together and his mouth was open. Bits of half-chewed ravioli were visible on his tongue. Tater waited for him to turn back to the television and discreetly gave him the finger, then looked guiltily up at me for approval.

"Let me see those clippers, Tate," I said, and snatched them out of his hand. I clamped his left nipple inside the little metal mouth and squeezed. I could feel the skin resist at first then quickly give way. It was harder to cut through than a fingernail but the sound of the metal mouth snapping together was louder and more satisfying. His eyes went wide. His pupils dilated. His jaw fell open. The blood ran down his chest and belly in a thick, oily stream, mixing with the dirt and the sweat and the tiny fuzzy hairs on his skin, and I threw up in my mother's sun-wilted rosebush while he screamed.

ANGELS

"WHEN YOU HEAR GABRIEL'S HORN A-BLOWIN'" it's gonna be too late," my mother said, when she wanted me to repent on my knees in front of her and her angels. Our trailer was covered with them. They were preening porcelain things posing with their eyes to God, their arms outstretched, their heads and shoulders flowing with thick gold locks of heavenly hair. They piled up in corners and along the kitchen counter, hovered over the toilet and stood in judgment atop the television set. She prayed for them to stand guard over us, to guide and protect us every day. In this way she was able to let us out of her sight. Clay jokes that when we broke into the trailers of sleeping neighbors, heavenly angels stood watch out front, and later, when we skipped school to skateboard in rain ditches and smoke cheap brown weed out of an empty soda can in the overgrown lot behind the Food Lion, heavenly angels held court all around us, catching us when we fell, blinding the eyes of patrolling officers, getting us miraculously high.

TREASURE

DAD BOUGHT OUR BUNK BEDS at a yard sale, brought them home in one piece in the back of the Ranger, took them apart in the yard, and with manly swagger dragged the pieces through the trailer and into the corner of our room, where he wordlessly reassembled them, grunting and sweating until it was finished, then said, "Gotcha some gall-dang bunk beds now," and dragged my old bed that he made with his own God-given hands before he knew me out to the Ranger and drove it away.

After hanging sheets from the top bunk and draping them all the way around to make a fort, Clay lay down on his back with his hands behind his head and told me that he stole things sometimes when he went out walking, that he slipped in through an open bedroom window or unlocked door and that he only ever took one thing. "In and out in thirty seconds," he said, "like a thief in the night." We both laughed at the phrase, one we'd picked up from the televangelist my mother watched when she got home from work, in the hours before Dad came rolling in, sweating and sunburned and in no mood for that kind of talk.

"What do you steal?" I asked.

"Treasure."

"What kind of treasure?"

He shrugged, "Just stuff, man. I'm gonna get one thing from every Goddamn trailer in this park."

"You'll never get anything from Shep's trailer," I said. He shrugged again and mumbled something under his breath. He'd hated Shep since the day he wandered up to the Milton trailer to see the statuary garden and gotten too close. When the security light kicked on Shep came rumbling out and said, "You got about half a second to get outta my yard before I knock you clear back to California." When Clay told the story, he quoted Shep with an exaggerated Texas drawl, and popped his head and shoulders and hips with every syllable, and I laughed so long and loud that Clay said if I didn't get a grip I was gonna pop a vein in my brain and keel over dead. The sound and shape of the phrase struck me as funny and I decided to keep it.

Clay looked at me with a smirk. "You ever seen a girl naked?" he asked. I thought about the brightly painted woman I'd seen in *National Geographic*, and about the summer before, when I accidentally shat myself at the babysitter's trailer, and hid my shit-filled Underoos inside the light fixture in her bathroom. She found them there, burning behind the bulb, shit smoke blinding her eyes as she dug them out with her fingertips, standing on the sink with her t-shirt over her mouth and nose, gagging. I stood just below her at the base of the sink and, looking up, I could see the dips and crevices of her vagina through the fabric of her bathing suit. Small blonde pubic hairs wound round its outer edges.

"Not really," I said, "not all the way."

"Hang on, I'll show you something," Clay said, and crawled out of the fort. I peeked through the sheets and watched him pull a duffel bag off the top shelf in the closet, unzip it, and rummage around. He pulled out a crumpled magazine and plopped it down in front of me.

"Have a look at this," he said, and tapped the cover with his finger. Its name escapes me now, but its lettering was a bright lusty red—*Busty* or *Top Heavy* or *Nymph*—and a wild mess of flesh was splashed across its cover. He flipped it open to a photo of a woman with blue hair, lips, fingernails, and nipples splayed out on a table. She wore a plastic translucent vest, also blue, and aimed a toy laser gun directly into the camera.

"That's what they look like," he said, and slapped me on the back. Later, when the blue-haired maiden had returned to her place among Clay's stolen treasures, I held the image of her in my mind and said a silent, yearning prayer for one chance to touch a woman like her.

THE WIDOW'S TRAILER

CLAY STOLE TWELVE SHINERS from Dad's stash in the shed. We drank them warm in the ditch behind the park, sitting on skateboards and smoking discarded cigarette butts without fear. We drank them fast, bottle for bottle, playing it cool and suppressing the urge to gag. After four beers Clay said watch this, and took his skateboard to the top of the ditch. He tried to drop in off its lip and fell hard on the concrete, bouncing and skidding and smacking his head. I laughed louder than I should have, made careless by the beers. He stood up quick, holding his head, and told me to touch my toes.

"Touch your Goddamn toes," he said, and I did, and he kicked me squarely in the behind. His aim was such that my eyes watered and my ears rang and afterward we sat quietly for a while on either side of the ditch, waiting for our pain to pass.

A mongrel dog wandered up the ditch and we poured Shiner on the concrete for him. He licked it up then sauntered along, wagging his tail and panting.

When we'd drank enough of the Shiners that we could carry the rest with us, we skated along the ditch with bottles sticking out of our pockets like joeys from kangaroo pouches. Now and again we popped out of the ditch to see what we could see. As the sun went down we took to peering into trailers, looking for an empty one with unlocked windows, but they were full of shirtless men with hairy shoulders and we were too drunk to rob anybody quietly.

After a while Clay said, "I know where there's a lady who sleeps naked by her window." He looked at me, solemn, with his eyebrows raised. "You can see her pretty good." We walked, holding our skateboards, to the edge of the park, over the chain-link fence at its perimeter, past the tree line and into the woods. The trailer was a silver single-wide parked in a clearing midway between the park and I-10, its wheels exposed and rotting. As we approached her window, Clay put his hand over my mouth and it reeked of the butts he'd smoked in the ditch.

"She's a sad old widow or somethin'," he whispered. "She sleeps all the time but she'll wake up if you try to touch her." I pried his hand from my face.

"I'm not gonna fucking touch her," I said. The word "fucking" came out louder than intended as it was my first curse and I'd been waiting for a reason to say it, biding my time since the night on the roof when I'd decided to do it, after I watched him shimmy down the oak outside our window and disappear. He led me around the far corner of the trailer to her bedroom window and looked in, then stepped away and motioned at me with a jerk of his head to stand where he had been.

I understood then why he warned me not to touch her, because I could have. There was no glass in her window and I could hear her breathing, see the rising and falling of her heavy breasts and the folds of dimpled flesh around her waist. I stared at her and loved her and wanted her. My head swam with the thrill of it, followed by my stomach, and I threw up in the grass outside the widow's trailer.

Clay led me home, laughing, not unkindly, and fetched me a ginger ale from the kitchen. "Go on and puke some more if ya need to," he said, and in the bathroom sink I puked up Shiners, concentrating on the drain. The room spun in woozy concentric circles around it but the drain stayed centered, like a pivot.

TATER TOT'S, NOT MINE

TATER TOT FOUND A DILDO at the bottom of the pool in the apartments where we walked sometimes at night and jumped the fence to swim naked in the dark. He brought it up from the deep end and waved it like Old Glory.

"What is it?" I asked, and instinctively ducked. He lobbed it at me, like I knew he would, and its pink skin glimmered. When it smacked against my cheek, like a fish hitting a butcher's block, I screamed, fearing AIDS or worse.

"Motherfucker!" I said, and scooped it up by its bulbous base. I chased him awkwardly through the water, wielding it over his head like the very Sword of Damocles.

"You should not have fucking done that," I said, then brought it down hard against his skull and face and finally, after prying open his lips and teeth with my fingers, shoved three quarters of it into his pleading mouth.

Thereafter I kept it like a talisman beneath my bunk. Secretly I measured my own manhood against its length and girth and found myself lacking.

Some weeks later my mother cleaned our room in a fit of giddy domesticity and found the cursed thing wedged among the action figures and comic books and plates of half-eaten food.

"What do you do with it?" she asked, her eyes watering, holding it out by her fingertips.

"It's Tater's," I pleaded. "He found it. He hit me with it."

"Why do you have it?"

"I took it away from him."

"Why did you keep it?"

"I don't know. For protection!"

"From what?"

"I don't know! Tater!"

"Tater's little. You're full of shit." When my mother cursed it was a shock. She had to force the word out through clenched teeth, as if it put her immortal soul in danger. "Get rid of it."

She chunked it at me and I picked it up and dropped it in the yellow Pac-Man trash can.

"Not there!" She shouted. "Get it out of here!"

I considered burying it in the yard but knew Buster would dig it up and bring it to Dad so that night I carried it back to the apartment pool where we swam and returned it to the depths from whence it came. I dropped it in without ceremony and it sank without a sound.

BROKEN ENGLISH

JUST AS THE SUN DIPPED behind the water tower, Lupe and Maria materialized in the street outside their trailer, fully formed, wearing oversized t-shirts and scuffed up plastic kneepads.

They held hands and skated in circles or figure eights, chanting "Ladies and Jelly Spoons" ("hobos and tramps, cross-eyed mosquitoes and bow-legged ants") or "Little Bunny Foo Foo," in broken, nearly indecipherable English. Clay and I stood on our skateboards in the street, drinking Diet Cokes from the fridge and belching manly from our guts for the girls to hear. They swung around us on their roller skates in ever tightening circles, orbiting faster and faster, closing in, giggling and chanting and clapping their hands. When they were close enough to touch, they clasped hands around us and spun, with us back to back between them, and sang or chanted some song or chant picked up from God-knows-where, "Got ya where we want ya, now we're gonna eat ya!" and they laughed and made gobbling noises and skated away.

We did this every night for a week, faithfully.

Afterward, we sometimes did tricks for them—ollies, curb slides, 360 to kickflips, and frontside power pop shove-its—but on this night Maria skated right up to Clay, took him by the wrist and led him away, toward the ditch behind our trailer, to do who-knows-what.

"Do you want to see?" Lupe said to me. "See?" I asked, and she said, "*Sí*," and laughed, and turned and skated back across the street to her trailer and opened the screen door and walked inside without taking off her skates. I stood swaying atop my skateboard, confused, staring after her.

The door swung open again, partially, and her head and fingers reappeared around its frame. Her smiling, disembodied head, hovering in the gloom, shouted, "Come see!" and the screen door fell shut again with a bang and her head and fingers were gone.

"Come in *joven!*" her mother shouted from the kitchen, and I stepped inside. It was dimly lit. There were thick rugs everywhere, and countless Christs suspended from crosses. Lupe's mother shouted something in Spanish and Lupe came bounding from her room in socks and walked right up to me and said "Hi," and held out her hand. I held out my own to her, thinking she meant to shake it, but she led me like a dog down the hall and into their room.

The girls' room was a feminized, Mexicanized version of ours. They slept in bunk beds, along the same wall, but theirs were covered in heavy colorful blankets. She spoke in a low, sweet voice, and I had a hard time understanding.

"Do you want to see?" she asked again.

"See?"

"*Sí?*" she said, "Do you want to see?"

"See what?"

She smiled and pulled what I took for a loosely bound book from atop a shelf beside their beds. She pulled me by the wrist again and we plopped down on the bottom bunk. The book was a photo album, the kind where the pictures are held haphazardly in place by static electricity and thin plastic sheets. It was full of Polaroids.

She opened the album to a picture of an old man with a white mustache at the foot of a set of concrete stairs dressed in a white flowing shirt, a purple skirt, a purple cape with pink trim decorated with tassels of every color, and huge leather boots covered with gold bulbs or bells dangling from strings and swinging wildly in every direction. On his head was a crown and from the back of the crown sprouted a plume of feathers, orange and white and pink and blue. There was a drum strapped to his belt he was beating with his left hand and in his right hand he held a bowl. He did not appear to be dancing. *"Eso es mi tío loco, Fabio,"* she said, and the words meant nothing to me, but their exact sound and shape mingled with the image of the old man and each to this day retain their mystery. The words, when spoken or privately thought, evoke the image of the old man and the smell of Lupe's hair in equal measure. *Eso es mi tío loco Fabio, Eso es mi tío loco Fabio, Eso es mi tío loco Fabio*: a prayer and a mantra and an incantation.

She flipped the page. I wanted to see it again but didn't know how to say so. She showed me a picture of chickens in cages piled atop one another in the street and one of dogs sleeping and one of her and Maria sitting next to an ancient woman on a bench, all three drinking through straws from plastic bags filled with some milky fluid. I wasn't sure what she was trying to show me.

She looked up from the book and gingerly reached a hand out to touch my curls. I produced a ring from my pocket I'd taken from my mother's dresser for just this purpose. It was a gold band shaped like Texas on top with a tiny diamond representing the capital pressed into its face. I tried to put it on her finger but it was too big. I slipped it onto her thumb instead. "Now you're my wife," I said, and she wiggled her thumb and held it up to the light.

She jumped up and dug under her bed, then pulled out an old Polaroid camera and aimed it at me. A whirring sound came from it, followed by the flash, blinding. We sat together with the developing picture between us, awed by its quiet magic. The picture caught me half turned away. She stuck it in her book, at the very end, then stood to put it back on the shelf. When she leaned over me a cross on a chain slipped free of her shirt and I touched it with my tongue. I thought wildly that Dad, sunburned and tired with his baseball and beer, had never done anything like that.

CEILING FANS

IN THE SUMMER, MOM SPOKE WISTFULLY of ceiling fans, but Dad had altogether more optimistic ideas. He wanted a door he didn't have to stoop through and a ceiling that he couldn't reach up and touch.

"Janey," he'd say, "I'm gonna get us a house here pretty soon. A big'un with a yard for old Buster and a kitchen big enough to cook in."

Dad's hair, curly and red, was permanently matted to his sunburned forehead. He wore a cap all day, climbing telephone poles and splicing lines with a set of wire cutters he kept in a leather holster slung low on his hip like a gunslinger—he pulled them out sometimes and spun them around his finger like a pistol, then slid them back in, a single fluid motion—and when he took that cap off, his hair stayed flat except below the cap line, where it puffed out in curls. He smelled always of sweat and dirt, the way men should. It is a matter of no small consequence to me that I have never in my life smelled quite that way.

When he slept, he looked like a giant infant with the head and hands of a man who worked in the sun. People in Texas are different than people in other parts of the world, especially redheaded people. They harden, like people made of clay.

BLACK CATS

TATER'S MOTHER TOOK TO SPENDING TIME with Shep Milton, who owned the park and Big Shep's Fireworks stand off Highway 10. For three weeks in the summer and three weeks before New Year's Eve, Shep stayed in an old RV parked behind the stand to keep kids from breaking in at night and stealing firecrackers. In the evenings, after working all day at the plant, Tater's mother picked Tater up from the babysitter's trailer and took him out to the fireworks stand, which sat just beyond the one and only Seaview exit, under the guise of providing him with the character-building experience of a summer job. While he worked the fireworks stand alone, Tater's mother and Shep disappeared into his RV until well after dusk, "making supper together," she told Tater. "Mr. Milton is Momma's friend. He's a nice man." After a while they brought out some reheated spaghetti or a bologna sandwich for him.

Without thought, I revealed all of this to Clay when he asked where Tater had been. "Why don't I ever see that shitty little kid?" he asked, and though Tater swore me to secrecy concerning his mother and Shep, I told Clay everything.

"What a slut," he said.

"She *is* a slut," I said, happy to place a face on a word I'd heard but didn't know. Clay hit on the idea of paying Tater a visit. We walked past Lupe and Maria sitting on the steps leading to their front door, listening to a *Tejano* station on a yellow boom-box and dancing with their heads and hands. We waved as we walked past and they waved back and smiled, Lupe demurely, Maria broadly and with teeth.

It took us half an hour to walk to the stand, the farthest I'd ever walked from home. It was a long wooden structure that sat a few feet from the service road and leaned forward at such an angle that I was inclined to stand back for fear of being crushed. It looked like a matchbook tossed away by a passing giant that landed on its side and stayed miraculously upright. Plastered at the corners of the sign that hung above the counter, a pair of snarling black cats framed the words "Big Shep's Fireworks" in faded red letters. Tater had his head on the counter. He appeared to be asleep.

I started to say Tater's name, but Clay put the palm of one sweaty hand over my mouth, put his finger to his lips with the other, and raised his eyebrows as high as they would go. He tiptoed up to Tater and put his head in close to listen to his breathing, then went around the side of the stand and peered at the RV parked behind it. The blinds over the RV's windows were drawn tight. Clay came back around to the front and with an elaborate series of hand gestures and eye movements indicated that I was to keep one eye on the RV and one on the service road to look out for anybody coming. He lifted himself over the counter of Big Shep's Fireworks and, once inside, proceeded to stuff his Velcro pockets and the inside of his pants with handfuls of cherry bombs, packages of Black Cats, a Catherine wheel, a Jack-in-the-Box and jumbo-sized bottle rockets. When he had as much as he could hold he climbed back over the counter and, holding his bulging Bugle Boys up with both hands, gestured with a nod that we should go.

Tater lifted his head. "Hey Cherry," he said, "Whatcha doin' here?" His bowl cut was in shambles where it had been cradled in his arms. A thin film of drool glistened against his cheek. He looked behind him at the wall filled with colorful explosives, seemed to remember where he was, and why, and put his head back down.

"Firecrackers, dip-shit, what do you think?" Clay said, and snorted.

"What kind you want?" Tater asked, without looking up. Clay put his elbows on the counter next to Tater's head and rested his chin in his hands. "Hmm," he said, "Let's see. Gimme some-a them smoke bombs and a couple of those big Roman candles." Tater had to scoot his stool against the wall and stand on it to reach the top shelf where the Roman candles were. Clay got a kick out of that so he waited for him to come back to the counter and sent him back up again for some silver jets, and then again for a grab bag he wanted to investigate. "Hey, how many pistol poppers are in that grab bag up top there?" he asked.

"I don't know," Tater whined, "Ith a grab bag. They're all different."

Clay wrinkled his forehead and Tater glanced at me

before climbing up again. I stood silently by with my legs crossed. I badly needed to pee. When he returned with the grab bag packaged with an image of a cartoon maiden bedecked in a star-spangled bikini straddling a rocket, Clay tossed it aside and said, "Get me some Black Cats, too." The Black Cats were easily accessible and Tater grabbed two packages and laid them with the pile on the counter.

"That all?" he asked.

Clay considered quietly for a moment, then said, "You ever stick a Black Cat up your ass and light it? I stuck a Black Cat up a cat's ass once, and lit it, and you should have seen that fucker. His hind legs came six inches up off the ground. I wonder what would happen if we stuck one up a little kid's ass and lit it. You think it'd blow your balls off?" Tater went stiff and Clay leaned in close, their faces almost touching. "What about your mom's ass? You think Big Shep is stickin' his big stick in your mom's ass right now?" Tater looked at me and Clay smacked him hard upside the head. "Don't look at him. You think he's your friend?"

Tater looked at his feet and held his breath to keep from crying. Clay hitched his britches up with one hand and turned to look at me. "Are you his friend, Cherry Tree? Cherry Tree and Tater Tot sittin' in a tree? F-U-C-K-I-N-G?" I glanced at the door of the RV, willing it to open, willing with my whole soul for Shep Milton to come barreling out and kick the shit out of Clay. I heard faint laughter from inside. "Are you his friend, Cherry?"

"No," I said.

"Good, cause I can't hang around with you if you're gonna be friends with little cry baby queers." He looked back at Tater and said, "Now, put all that shit back." I followed him home, holding my crotch in my hands.

THE ABANDONED TRAILER

I FOUND MY WAY BACK to the widow's trailer beyond the tree line, and saw the words "Tow Away" scrawled in paint along the skirting. I peeked through the window where I'd seen the sleeping widow, and instead saw an empty room piled with garbage and abandoned furniture. I crawled inside. It was hot and dank and smelled of a deep, indefinable rot. The smell was a living thing. Breathing though your mouth, you could taste it. In the living room, a busted La-Z-Boy sat amid chunks of particleboard and cotton candy swirls of shining pink insulation. In the kitchen, I sat for a while on an overturned pot and stared into an ancient oven full of rusted metal teeth and the charred remnants of a thousand meals. I wondered if anything good had ever come from it. I wondered if I should show Clay or keep it for myself. I wondered if the vision of the widow in the window had only been a dream brought on by the Shiners, summoned by the shadows and the power of suggestion.

There were baseboards everywhere, with rusty nails pointing up. Being barefoot, I stepped carefully back to the window and crawled back through into daylight.

I regretted telling Clay about the trailer like I have regretted so many things, instantly. We spent a few hours scrounging around closets and cupboards for something salvageable but the trailer itself was the only thing. In the freezer Clay found the source of the smell. A writhing carpet of mold and maggots covered a box of raw hamburger patties. Its cardboard container was soggy with blood and busted along the seams, unable to contain both the rotting meat and the squirming millions. Clay laughed and covered his nose with his shirt. "Don't that stink a bitch!" he shouted, and backed away, waving his free arm in front of him. I caught sight of the mess and felt myself gagging, felt my traitorous stomach readying to spill. I made it as far as the window we'd crawled in, but failed to get my head through before it came up in a violent spray that splattered down the wood panel and gathered in a puddle on the carpet.

We came back by the cover of night. We took off our shirts and wet them with a hose and tied them around our heads to cover our noses and mouths, then wrestled with the refrigerator, dragging it through the trailer's busted screen door and depositing it, finally, just beyond the tree line with all the abandoned couches and busted television sets. The clearing around the trailer was overgrown and unrecognizable metal fragments seemed to grow up from the ground alongside sunflowers, crabgrass, and weeds. Every night we crawled out through our window and strode back with giddy purpose to secretly clean and restore our abandoned trailer in the dark.

The only thing we left was the busted La-Z-Boy

because, we figured, we'd need a place to sit, but in the end Clay decided it would be his throne and forbade me to use it.

"I don't wanna sit on the dang thing anyway," I said. "Prolly got fleas."

One by one we brought in things from home, comics and posters and my mother's plants, secreted away in the night. Clay brought his stolen treasures and arranged them around the trailer according to some secret logic. He stored the fireworks stolen from Shep beneath the kitchen sink.

I brought a small wicker rocking chair I'd had since time immemorial, so I'd have somewhere to sit. "This is my throne," I said. "Don't even think about sittin' on it," and he sat on it, to prove himself, but he was too big and when he tried to rock he broke its arms and back.

Clay hit on the idea of taking Maria there to make out. He lured and plied her with Shiners stolen from Dad's stash. I secretly followed and spied them through a busted window. He was sitting on the puffy chair and Maria was sprawled out on his lap with her legs dangling over the left arm. Her shirt was off and one of her tiny brown breasts was in his open mouth. His left hand was dug in between her legs. The vision of them coupled there on the puffy chair was all too much and I ducked beneath the window. Listening to the urgent sounds they made, I thought of the battalion of angels gathered round, dispatched by my mother, and wondered if they covered their ears. I stayed hunkered beneath the window and stole peeks at them until Clay picked her up with a strength that had sex in it and carried her into the bathroom.

I crossed my legs in the weeds and wished I had a cigarette to puff on or a half a can of Shiner.

SHEEP

"I SHOW YOU A PLACE," I SAID TO LUPE. Unconsciously, I sometimes mimicked her broken English when we talked, thinking, probably, that she would understand me better that way. She took her camera from beneath her bed and hung it by its strap from her neck.

While we walked she took my hand in hers and I wished I knew a poem to say or that I had a voice like Elvis to croon her a song. Instead I nervously told jokes memorized from Laffy Taffy wrappers and pointed out significant places. "That there's Tater's trailer," I said. "He lives there with his crazy ol' mamma." Lupe took a picture.

"You know what's a ghost's favorite ice cream?" I asked, watching as she shook the Polaroid, and then slid it into her bag without waiting for it to develop. "Booberry!"

It was getting on to dusk as I led her up to Shep's trailer. A stone-cut ram and statuary sheep had appeared on the only patch of unoccupied grass in front of the brightly painted doublewide. The sheep were disproportionately larger than the other stone animals in the yard. They looked regal among the smaller cows and pigs and chickens. We approached them on tippy toe, until the pair of lights attached to the trailer came to life and flooded the scene.

We froze, then scurried away like rats and hid behind a juniper bush.

"It's ok," I whispered. "Shep's not here." We sat Indian style on a patch of crabgrass, and stared. Lupe's foot grazed the rough bottom of my own and she left it there. She whispered *mira* and pointed with her eyes. Mrs. Milton stood in the doorway cradling a finely wrought lamb in her matronly arms. It lay with its legs folded, like in a painting of Christ the Shepherd. She moved through the screen door, still cradling the lamb, and glided down the steps onto the path of colored glass that led to the bushes behind which we sat with the bottoms of our bare feet touching. Mrs. Milton's feet were also bare, and by the glow of the security light her nightgown appeared to flow from her body like the smoke that flowed eternally from the chimney of the plant where every adult I knew worked, except for her and Shep and Dad.

Mrs. Milton laid the lamb at the feet of the ewe, clapped her hands together, and went inside.

"*Una ovejita*," Lupe said, and tittered.

CICADAS

ON THE MORNING OF THE DAY I cut Tater's nipple off, five days after the tornado and three days after the 4th of July, Clay woke me with a smack, rolled me over, pulled my arms behind my back, tied them together at the wrist using a length of rolled up pillowcase, and tied my feet together using his bed sheet with a knot between my ankles. The remainder of the sheet hung loosely between my legs and he used it to drag me off my bunk and through the trailer like a mule pulling a cart. My face and exposed belly burned across the carpet.

He kicked open the screen door and dragged me onto the wooden porch without slowing. My chin and bottom lip smacked the bottom of the door frame and I bit my tongue when my head bounced against the lower surface of the porch. My mouth filled with blood and the taste reminded me of the warm pennies Clay had fed me from his own pocket while perched on my chest in the yard one morning after he'd fed me grass and bits of sticks and the wings of a June Bug that stuck in my throat and reminded me of the flecks of microwaved popcorn that Dad made for dad-gum movie nights and Ranger games. Clay hesitated on the porch and looked up and down the empty street.

"Don't pull me down those stairs, Clay," I pleaded with him. "I'll die."

"OK," he said, and rolled me off the side of the porch into the rose bush at its base. I lay gasping among the thorns and sun-wilted roses. Clay walked down the stairs, picked the linen train from the bush, and dragged me out.

Who knows how long it took him to string me up in that tree? Civilizations could have risen and fell, oceans formed, the universe could have ceased to expand. In the time it takes a cicada to shed its skin, he could have lifted me up by my feet, flung the length of sheet that hung below me over the thick part of a low-hanging limb, and strung me up by my ankles. Time had lost its shape but I swear to God I watched his shadow lengthen.

My Superman Underoos t-shirt hung about my armpits and face, partly obscuring my view, but I could hear him snap open his homemade switchblade and cut two twigs from the end of the branch from which I swung, then test them against the hide of the tree. They were dry and hard but not completely dead so they had some give. I had rotated away from him when I felt the first sting against the exposed skin at the small of my back, and I thought fleetingly that an errant cicada was feeding on me, but it was followed by a hail of others that came faster and with more ferocity as he found his stride. The individual blows were almost bearable, but the sting of each blow piled atop the previous one and was magnified. I became aware of three sounds simultaneously, a high-pitched whine coming from myself, a stream of aimless vulgarity from Clay, and the choral swell of the cicadas in the tree, growing ever louder in their mindless sexual frenzy.

When he'd worn himself out, he untied my hands and sawed through the sheet binding my feet to the tree with his switchblade, lowered me to the ground, then sat again with his heavy butt on my chest. He leaned in close and pressed his index finger against my forehead. With hot, rancid breath on my face, I heard him plainly say, "You are not my brother," then he stood up and walked inside.

I lay beneath the tree and listened to it hum. The very air around me vibrated with the song of the cicadas. I imagined that I could hear each of them individually rattling from their pod-bearing limbs. I pretended I was dead, and that the blood in my mouth was a sacramental wine. Who knows how long I lay beneath that tree, trying not to move or blink or breathe? When the cicadas were quiet, I gathered up the remnants of Clay's pillowcase and bed sheet, and went inside.

I dug around under my bunk until I found Lupe's picture book, took it into the bathroom, and laid it among the angels on top of the toilet. I turned on the bathwater as hot as it would go and poured shampoo into the stream until the tub filled with bubbles. I took off my t-shirt, but I kept my red underwear on to guard against the sting of the hot water on my privates. The welts on my back and chest burned temporarily brighter, but dulled as I lay there. I scooped some suds from the water, plopped them down on my head, and shaped my curls into shampoo horns the way my mother always had. I picked up Lupe's book from atop the toilet and turned to the pictures she'd shown me. Lupe, who showed me pictures, who laughed at my jokes, who touched my hair and feet. Lupe, who slept through the tornado in the abandoned trailer, unharmed, and crawled that very night with her mother and sister into the back of a truck driven by a brown man in a greasy ball cap with a black mustache that rhymed with that of the old man in the picture wearing a feathered crown and cape and boots with bells or tassels, each of them carrying bags of clothes and food salvaged from their trailer that had been spun off its wheels and thrown headlong into a gully. When they were gone we rummaged through their abandoned things and Clay found Lupe's picture book. I convinced him to trade it for a toy switchblade I found with a comb where the blade went that he replaced with a real blade taken from a kitchen knife and carried in his back pocket, for protection.

"*Eso es mi tío loco, Fabio,*" I said to the picture, and I imagined that Lupe and Maria and their mother were back with Fabio and the old lady and the chickens and dogs. I knew that even if I went there, I would never find her.

Clay sat in front of the television, watching cartoons. I took a can of Chef Boyardee from the cupboard and poured it into a pot, then set the pot on the stove and poured two glasses of milk. I poured chocolate from a spout into the milk, let it settle at the bottom of the glasses, stirred it with a dirty spoon. Water dripped from my feet and Underoos. I spooned the ravioli into two bowls and carried the rations into the living room. I laid Clay's food and milk in front of him and he ate without looking at me. Just as I sat down, there was a knock at the door. Clay didn't move or look around or make any kind of movement at all. I stood up again, opened the door, and there stood Tater, shirtless, picking dirt from his nails with a set of metal clippers.

PARA TI

"I'LL SHOW YOU ANOTHER PLACE," I said to Lupe, and she turned and ran into her trailer. The screen door swung shut behind her and I stood squinting to see through it. She returned, finally, with her camera hanging from her neck. "Ready," she said, in perfect, practiced English.

At the abandoned trailer I showed her where the words "Tow Away" were scrawled along the base and she took a picture. "You know where cats go for their class trip? The meow-seum." Inside, I showed her the La-Z-Boy recliner and she took a picture. "How does the man on the moon get his hair cut? Eclipse it." I showed her where we kept the stolen fireworks and the remnants of our stolen Shiners. I opened one by holding the wedged lip of the cap against the edge of the kitchen counter and smashing it with my fist, like an old pro, and held it out to her. She drank it quick, in big gulps, and belched deeply from her belly.

"*Pelirrojo*," she said, and laughed, and touched the crown of my head. "*Sin zapatos, Pelirrojo.*" She sounded like an Indian chief from the dad-gum John Wayne films Dad half watched on Sunday afternoons, drifting in and out of sleep, splayed like an infant on his recliner.

She walked quietly around the trailer, touching things

and taking pictures. Her short fingernails looked eaten off but were painted a sparkling blue. I opened the bathroom door and made her sit on the rotten tiles, then, with a magician's flair, I threw back the shower curtain to reveal the lamb cut from stone, resting in a bed of grass and leaves I collected from the yard and carefully arranged at the base of the tub. I smiled and held one hand out to the lamb and one to her.

Her eyes widened at the sight of it, her lips parted.

"*Para ti*," I said.

KNIVES

A LITTLE WHILE AFTER CUTTING OFF HIS NIPPLE, I walked across the street to see for sure that Tater wasn't dead. The front door of his trailer stood open, so I pulled open the screen door without knocking and stepped inside. Blankets hung over the windows and the only light in the room came from the small television that sat atop a larger television flickering silently in the corner. A record ran endlessly on its runout groove. I stood in the doorway waiting for my eyes to adjust. Something was on the floor in front of the stereo, and I moved closer, fearing it was Tater, but it was his mother laid out amid a pile of Elvis and Beach Boys records. It was Hell-hot and the air was thick with smoke. Cigarettes were piled in ashtrays and stuffed into empty cans. Tater's mother lay noisily breathing at the foot of the record player, clutching a plastic vodka bottle to her chest. I pried it from her fingers and sniffed it. It smelled of hospital corridors and clean, sharp knives. She wore a loose-fitting t-shirt with the sleeves cut off and her left breast was partially exposed where it hung down toward her armpit. I lifted the cloth of the shirt to get a better look. A jagged scar wound round the bottom, up toward the nipple.

"Thtop lookin' at her," Tater said.

He was standing in the hallway outside his room, holding a ball of wadded up toilet paper to his chest.

"I'm sorry, Tate," I said.

"You're a thunofabitch," he shouted, "just like your athole brother." I felt a white-hot rush of pride, mixed with shame, but I couldn't think of how to respond so I didn't say anything. He stood breathing and bleeding through his ball of tissue, staring at me as I hovered over his prostrate mother, then he sat on the floor and started to cry.

"Lemme see," I said, and motioned for him to move the toilet paper. The area around where his nipple had been was swollen and purple. I poured vodka on it and he howled like a wounded dog.

"You got any Band-Aids?" I asked him. He looked around at the piles of boxes and newspapers stacked around the room.

"Probly thumwhere," he said.

I said, "Stay right here," and ran back down the hall and through the living room, out the front door and back across the street to our trailer where the Band-Aids were kept always on a tiny shelf behind the mirror in the bathroom along with antiseptic and gauze in a white tin with a red cross on it, bought with love and placed there by my mother in case of emergencies.

I grabbed the tin and sprinted back across the street to Tater, who was lying face up on the floor, a tiny emaciated echo of his mother, holding the bloody tissues to himself and not crying at all. I lifted the tissue and applied the ointment from the tube, then stuck five Band-Aids over his wound, one on top of the other in the shape of a star.

FLIGHT

LIGHTNING FLASHES OUTSIDE the bathroom window and before I can count to one-Mississippi its attendant thunder shakes the trailer and makes ripples in my bathwater. Mom hops up from the edge of the tub and hands me a towel. "Dry yerself 'n git dressed," she says. From the living room I can hear through a wall of static the disembodied voice of the weatherman. Dad yells "Janey," and she leaves me bleeding in the bathtub with soap in my eyes. I hear the screen door open and close and open and close again.

The siren, when it starts, scares me more than the weather. I think that it must be Gabriel blowing his horn, and I know that I know that I know I'll be left behind. Without rinsing or drying off I put on my Underoos and tie a towel around my neck, then run outside. The whole street is standing in the rain, staring at the sky.

Necks go stiff from looking up. Nerves are shot. Beers are opened. Neighbors who never speak stand together in each other's lots, drinking and praying. I run shirtless and barefoot through sheets of rain. No one tries to stop me. The sky churns and churns. I'm convinced that if I run fast enough the swirling currents will lift me by my cape and carry me to the sky.

Maria and her mother are wandering the street looking for Lupe, calling her name over and over, but the wind rises and falls and snatches their voices from their mouths. I do not tell them that I left her in the abandoned trailer, that she fell asleep in the tub nuzzled at the feet of the stolen stone-cut lamb after drinking two of Dad's Shiners, that I noticed she wasn't wearing the ring shaped like Texas and pressed with a diamond where the capital goes so I woke her and asked her why not and she said, groggily, "*Lo siento,* my mom say it's too nice, she take it to your mom." I don't admit that I left her there, running at top speed, and leapt over the chain-link fence that cut my stomach or that I bled through my shirt and when I got home it looked as though I'd been shot. I do not say that my mother instantly forgave me and took off my shirt and put it in the sink to soak and put me in the bath and washed my wound and my hair and baptized me with water from a plastic cup.

A finger emerges from the swirling cloud, stretching and yawning and reaching for dirt. The park gasps.

"Lord God," says Tater's mother, and my mother takes her by the hand and prays.

The wind picks up and Shep comes barreling into the park in his pickup, throwing up gravel and honking. "Git in the ditch!" he shouts, and we run like a herd of startled deer and pile into an expanse of concrete ditch, eight feet deep, and we huddle together and put our heads between our knees. Maria drags her frantic mother into the ditch and holds her down to keep her from running back out.

Mrs. Milton, in her nightgown and slippers, is holding onto Shep. Tater's mother has him wrapped up so tight he's squirming and complaining and struggling to breathe. Tina, visibly pregnant now, makes her way gingerly into the ditch with her mother guiding her at the hips. Clay and Dad are bravely standing together at the lip of the ditch, watching the sky. Dad calls out to Buster and Buster comes running. My mother finds me and covers me with her body and we wait. I imagine dying here, being crushed alongside all these people by a truck or a tree or a flying metal trailer. I imagine everybody being swept up together into the sky and spinning and screaming and holding onto each other's hands. I wonder where we would land. I wonder if we would be the same or if all our clothes would be mixed up and maybe we wouldn't know who we were or be able to find our way back.

The wind picks up again and a sound comes screaming down on our heads like Gabriel's trumpet and the end of everything. I look over my mother's shoulder and stare out at the sky beyond the ditch. I keep tally of the things that fly by: trash can, lawn chair, a pink flamingo with a missing head. Through the noise I hear my mother fervently praying for the protection of angels, that He would send them to encamp themselves round about this ditch and our trailer, until the roar of the storm begins to fade and the sound of her prayers and sobs and the murmuring and sobbing of the others is all I hear. I struggle to free myself and climb out of the ditch and she claws after me and tells me no, but I have to see. The finger is withering and receding. The rain has stopped. It's quiet.

Others climb up from the ditch and gather in the street. The sky is clear and bright and hard to look at. The sky is full of knives, pointing down.

Trailers are piled atop one another, upside down and inside out, crushed like tin cans, pulled apart like accordions. For a moment it is silent in the ditch, silent in the park. For a breathless moment that seems to stretch out in front of us in every direction a perfect, heavy silence holds sway.

If God or the angels would have looked down at the A-1 mobile home park in the minutes after the tornado, he or they would have seen two rows of trailers that zigzagged and overlapped in crazy, unpredictable patterns. He or they would have seen gaps in the rows like missing teeth in a rotten mouth, and he or they would have seen me running through them in bare feet and Underoos, my cape billowing in the wind, back to the abandoned trailer beyond the tree line, with Lupe's mother and sister and my mother and Clay and Buster following just behind.

BOTTLE ROCKETS

AT DUSK ON JULY 4TH, 1987, two days after the tornado, the A-1 trailer park was still without electricity, and the trailers themselves lay mostly in ruins.

"We pray hard, work hard, fight hard," Mom said. "And one day God grabs us by the neck and shakes 'til all our bones are broke and we can't no more than even try to move, and he does it, I think, so we know that we know that we know that we're nothin' without Him." She said it with the conviction of a true believer and the bitterness of a long battered wife. "I shoulda prayed for the protection of all the trailers," she added. "I was selfish."

With a flashlight in his mouth, Clay opened our bedroom window and crawled outside. I followed just behind him, and we slipped back to the abandoned trailer in the dark. The front door hung open and Clay retrieved his bag of stolen firecrackers from under the sink, where they'd remained undiscovered, then we climbed an oak with a branch thick enough to hold us that overhung the trailer's roof, and shimmied along it until we could touch the trailer with our toes. Clay set up the Catherine wheel in the very center of the roof, lit a stolen cigarette, puffed, then used its smoldering tip to light the fuse. The

Catherine wheel started to spin. Sparks flew off into the night and from their meager light Tater materialized in the darkness below. "What are y'all doin'?" he asked in a giddy stage whisper.

"Celebrating," Clay bellowed back. Then he lit the Jack-in-the-Box and it bounced and fizzed across the roof and fell into a mess of leaves near the windowless window where I'd seen the sleeping widow or dreamed her dreaming ghost. Tater ran forward and stomped it out with a flip-flopped foot. "If Thep catcheth ya'll he'll know you're the oneth took them firecrackerth," Tater said. Clay lit a string of Black Cats and dropped them on Tater's head. Then, as a grand finale, he lit all three bottle rockets. They screamed, and shot straight up in the air. Even Tater gasped. Multicolored balls of fire scattered in all directions and then exploded as they dropped. We ooh'd and ah'd while wave after wave of luminous fury danced around our heads.

ABOUT THE AUTHOR

AARON TEEL hails from Austin, Texas, and is currently an MFA fiction fellow at Washington University in St. Louis. His work has appeared previously in *Tin House, Smokelong Quarterly, Monkeybicycle, Brevity,* and others. His novella-in-flash *Shampoo Horns* won the Rose Metal Press Sixth Annual Short Short Chapbook Contest in 2012.

4 | MARGARET PATTON CHAPMAN

Writing the Novella-in-Flash:
Maps, Secrets, and Spaces In-Between

Bell and Bargain

WRITING THE NOVELLA-IN-FLASH:
MAPS, SECRETS, AND SPACES IN-BETWEEN

1. TREASURED MAPS

"A story or novel is a kind of map because, like a map, it is not a world but evokes one."

—PETER TURCHI,
MAPS OF THE IMAGINATION

A number of years ago in Chicago, the artist and geographer Daniel Tucker, along with a Chicago-based collective of radical cartographers, started the People's Atlas project. Their magazine, *Area*, published a blank outline of the city of Chicago and invited people to fill in the map as they saw fit. I had just begun teaching at the time and was working where I could: poetry in elementary schools in the mornings, fiction after school to high school students, and college composition at night. I made copies of the map and took them everywhere, asking my students to fill in the blanks, to draw or write or label the city as they saw it. I gave them colored pencils and markers and half an hour or so. The elementary students almost always drew their houses, their streets, sometimes their schools, filling up almost all of the space, ignoring streets in-between. The high school students were more precise, attempting scale and adding more places of importance. College students either went for detail and accuracy, putting tiny buildings downtown, the river, the school, or they totally eschewed traditional geographical representation, allowing the map to contain personal histories, fears, or future goals. This map-making seemed to have important parallels to writing, but I was not sure why or how. It seemed that these maps revealed hidden cities all around me, other people's cities.

It wasn't until I read Peter Turchi's *Maps of the Imagination: The Writer as Cartographer* that I discovered language to put to the intuition I had about the map as narrative and narrative as map. The story, like the map, is only one way of evoking a world based on certain constraints. One could make a Chicago of the intersecting and looping blue highways, or the multicolored lines of the "L" marching in formation, or the web of thin, black bike paths, or the patchwork quilt of aldermen's districts; one could make a Chicago like a child's home, sprawling across neighborhoods, straddling the river, tumbling into the lake. None of these is strictly accurate in its description of the city; none could be. Cartography fails us the same way narrative does—the same way language does, of course. It is a useful approximation of something, but its utility is only in its inaccuracies: what it does not show, what it omits and hides in order that we may see what the mapmaker or storyteller thinks necessary.

Like an explorer, I started writing *Bell and Bargain*

without much idea as to its potential form. Like most writers, probably, I started writing because I was excited about characters and the worlds they lived in. I wrote small pieces as they came to me, and the stories evolved. I did not conceive of this work as a novella-in-flash, per se, until the opportunity to submit to Rose Metal Press presented itself. I had, however, conceived of this work in a number of different ways: as fragmented fiction, as traditional narrative, as an epic novel or series of novels, as poetry (including a cycle of sonnets), and as a novella. I was working on some of this writing in graduate school, and in one class my instructor, Janet Desaulniers, drew it for me as a tree, a dozen or so pieces of letter-sized paper taped together, and so it also exists as a map-tree. Each of the pieces of this work came out as little bits, glimpses and fragments, each a clue to the story but each mysterious even for me. I tried for a long time to make them into something big. In the form of the novella-in-flash, they are allowed to be both small and big. It seemed to me, and still does, that a number of maps might be made of this territory, but this form gave me a set of constraints within which to map the story of the girl Bell and her family.

2. THE SPACE OF EMPTY SPACE

> "Whereas the short story limits material and the novel extends it, the novella does both in such a way that a special kind of narrative structure results, one which produces [...] the double effect of intensity and expansion."
>
> —JUDITH LEIBOWITZ,
> *NARRATIVE PURPOSE IN THE NOVELLA*

How important is it to identify forms, to name them? Names categorize but they can also isolate. There are real consequences, I think, of calling something a novella, at least today, at least in publishing, which might be why it is so difficult to find new novellas right now. If you look for a list of novellas that embrace the form, you'll find the old cast of high-school English favorites—*Ethan Frome, Of Mice and Men, The Turn of the Screw, Bartleby, the Scrivener, The Time Machine*, etc.—books I mostly couldn't stand the first time I was required to read them, a number of which I still dislike.

But there are tons of novellas around, often hidden in plain sight. Until recently, Amazon had a "text stat" feature that allowed readers to see how many words were in a book; it was removed a year or so ago, I assume at the behest of publishers, or writers, who feared readers might use it to question book pricing. I loved it, because it revealed the secret lengths of books. Discovering how many words someone's book contains can feel like finding out the size of their take-home pay, or even more intimate knowledge, and Amazon's feature was revealing. People are publishing novellas, novellas that I love, sneaking in formal otherness where they can: the chapbook, the short story collection, the novel filled with open spaces.

One of the most important of these secret novellas to me is Jeanette Winterson's *Weight*, a retelling of the story of Atlas and Herakles for the Cannongate Myths series. It careens through time and space, switches point of view, and gets interrupted by the author herself. It is a history of histories of the universe, beginning with the Big Bang and ending in the future, and it is under 20,000 words. Plenty of works I love might be novellas even if they don't identify as such. Robert Coover's haunting *Briar Rose* is 96 pages and often called a novel; Azareen Van Der Vliet Oolomi's dark and insistent *Fra Keeler* is barely over a hundred pages in print. Claire Vaye Watkins' devastating "The Diggings" is 60 pages and a short story. Heather Cousin's *Something in the Potato Room*, which looks like a novella crafted from a series of very short stories, considers itself a collection of poetry, as does Michael Ondaatje's *The Collected Works of Billy the Kid*, which was very influential on my early drafts of this novella. Formally, Sarah Shun-Lien Bynum's *Madeleine Is Sleeping* feels like a novella-in-flash. It is over 200 print pages, but so is Kelcey Parker's full, surprising, and lovely *Liliane's Balcony: A Novella of Fallingwater*. Shun-Lien Bynum's novel does the work of intensity and expansion which Leibowitz speaks to, each section settling in its blankness. It is also about a magical young woman, but the opposite of Bell, a young woman caught in dreams. Each of these novellas is concerned with myth, with secrets, and with the magic of madness; each allows space for the unreal, something I think the novella, and the novella-in-flash, are particularly suited for.

The compressed space and bite-sized narratives of this form allowed me to tell quite a long story time-wise, from birth to adolescence, and to explore a number of characters in ways I think would be difficult in a more traditional form. Like a map's, a narrative's omissions shape its picture of a world. The novella-in-flash is a form of omission and lacuna. Words do not always fill pages, pages do not make much heft. Both on the page and in the narrative, it is a form of emptiness and white space, or as Melville meditated, of "dumb blankness, full of meaning, in a wide landscape of snows." Each of the individual pieces in *Bell and Bargain* gestures to more than there is on the page. However, the form also allows that this gesture is insufficient, because writing is insufficient, because, as Gaston Bachelard points out in *The Poetics of Space*, "[a]ll we communicate to others is an orientation towards what is secret without ever being able to tell the secret objectively." Bell is allowed to not dream in a sea of blankness. I hope also that that blankness resonates with the readers in its terribleness; one of the largest blanks in the story is the space that would explain how and why the baby Bell speaks.

3. SILENCE AND DANGER

> "The first word you utter will pierce through the hearts of your brothers like a deadly dagger. Their lives hang upon your tongue. Remember all I have told you."
>
> —HANS CHRISTIAN ANDERSEN,
> "THE WILD SWANS"

Bell is very much a character from a fairy tale: the wished-for daughter, the youngest, the magical child. Her story and character are influenced by two famously voiced and silenced young women from classic fairy tales: the Little Mermaid and the princess sister from a number of versions of the Swan Brothers tale. Both are tragic figures who seem to give away their voices for men. Both also point to the relationships between self and voice and demonstrate how dangerous the world can be for an unvoiced woman; both characters make trades that end in barely redeemed tragedies.

In her essay "Fairy Tale Is Form, Form Is Fairy Tale" Kate Bernheimer describes formal aspects employed by writers of classic fairy tales and how they can function in contemporary writing. Of the four fundamental aspects to fairy tale writing she identifies—flatness, abstraction, intuitive logic, and normalized magic—the first three might be defined as the absence of something that traditional realism demands: flatness, the absence of psychological depth in characters; abstraction, the absence of concrete imagery or detailed description;

intuitive logic, the absence of rational causal connection between events. Only the last of these, normalized magic, requires an addition: the magic in fairy tales that is so integral and ubiquitous as to be unremarkable, both to characters and to the reader. Each of these stylistic moves informs my writing and much of the writing I'm drawn to, and I think the novella-in-flash is well suited to both abstraction and intuitive logic, i.e., a lack of description and a lack of explanation.

Perhaps this willingness to allow omission is why the form lends itself to the unreal and magical. Lacunae make space for normalized magic because emptiness is inaccessible and cannot be questioned. These intimate spaces of unknowing are important meeting places for reader and writer, places of mystery. Here, yes, very well might be monsters. And children accept this sort of intimate unknowing, if we accept that fairy tales are for children, and there are no explanations for why a sister must silently sew shirts to redeem her brothers from lives as birds. Similarly, Bell's strangeness does not offer explanation. The lack of it assures us that her world is not the same as ours. Perhaps the novella-in-flash also need to offer no explanation except that it is what it is: glimpses of secrets, artifacts and clues; a map not to but of treasures; small things pieced together into a whole.

—MARGARET PATTON CHAPMAN

BELL AND BARGAIN

BY MARGARET PATTON CHAPMAN

TABLE OF CONTENTS

BIRTH

ON THE DAY OF HER BIRTH, she opened her mouth and instead of a cry or a gurgle or a precocious giggle, she spoke her name. It was the first mystery of her life, this self-naming, in September of 1884. Her father would not have liked the name she gave herself, but her father was not there; he'd left Chicago for Montana to pound the line through. Her mother was alone with two sons, alone to give birth with the help of female neighbors in the back bedroom of the squat brick house, in a neighborhood of dark and crowded bunched-up two-flats on the south side of the city.

The mother, on her own, intended to give the child one of the names agreed on by her absent common-law husband. A boy was to be Arthur, after the mother's father, having already passed on the father's family names to two sons. For a girl, the mother favored Fanny, the name of her own mother, but the father wished for the more modern sounding Dorothy, hoping someday to call her Dotty, a name that bespoke the promise of the next century, with its ticks and tacks, its coded electric signals. Dots and dashes and lines drove through.

The labor was hard. The mother thought that births got easier as you had more, and her second boy had taken less time than the first. But the girl was slow in coming. In the close air of the big room on the ground floor, curtains closed, stove lit for water, the mother sweat and bled and shat. Her water broke in the parlor, soaking her dress, her underthings, and the rough carpet with fluid, sweet and salty smelling. Holding her belly to relieve the pressure between her legs and on her unnamable inner parts, she walked to the front door and called out to the first person she saw, a five-year-old girl named Annie, to get the women who dealt with these things, and say that the baby was on its way.

When the girl was born, late and fat, when her chubby shoulders were through by pushing and the rest of her was pulled swiftly out and the cord cut and the afterbirth burnt in the fire and the sheets pulled off and with the newly stained chenille cover put in a tub out back to be washed, without asking, by the neighbors, and new sheets and blanket put on the still damp bed and the little girl wrapped up in a soft cloth diaper and the little crochet hat that the mother had made located and placed on her bald head, the baby took to tit and drank. The feeding was easier with the third child than the first two because her nipples had swollen and elongated and the thick liquid of her first milk passed easily through the mother's skin.

After the birth and her first meal, in the calm of the dawn of her first day, with her little head still funny shaped from coming out and laying on her mama's bosom, the baby said her name, clear and ringing as the word itself.

"Bell," she said.

The neighbor women had left to their own homes and the boys were off with an old woman who gave them candy and put a poultice on Abe's face, and so the mother was the only one who heard. Alone, the mother considered what her infant had just done, her breath lifting the child on her chest, one hand under the baby's bottom and one laid gently on her neck.

She considered and simply, softly, and without question said "Bell."

"Bell," said Bell, the tip of her new tongue flicking the dental "L" off of her toothless gums.

"Yes," said her mother, but she wondered.

The bells of the new day sounded, and the mother held Bell to her and the newness of the baby girl, flesh loose on small, soft bones, put a sweet pressure on her heart.

BEGINNINGS

BELL DOES NOT REMEMBER what she was thinking when she learned to speak.

She does not remember the way language formed in her, or the answers she gave to any of the questioners who sought her out for her mystical knowledge. Her brother Paul would ask her why she had named herself Bell. At four she answered because it was her name. At nine she had said it must have been the first word she heard. At thirteen-and-a-half, as their mother lay dying, Bell admitted that she did not know. Like most of us, she could not remember anything about her infancy; the baby Bell was as foreign and unknowable to her as the other side of the sky. She did wonder, while tending her mother, how it was that she came into her ordinary and inescapable present from such a miraculous, if forgotten, past.

BROTHERS

BELL'S BROTHERS, SEVEN AND FIVE, heard from the neighborhood children that their mother was to finally have the baby and knew this gave them leave to be out as long as they wanted so they went to look at the alley chickens and to beg sweets off old women who lived by themselves.

Abe and Paul, in their plus-fours, their pedal pushers, in what their maternal grandmother would have called "breeches" and their paternal grandmother "britches," in their machine-knit socks and machine-woven canvas jackets, in their hand-knit sweaters, squatted down in an alley and, with hands on knees like inspectors looking at pressure gauges, inspected chickens. When Abe, the younger one, went after a baby chick, the mother hen jumped at him and scratched his face. Paul pulled the chicken off and in his first infantile act of heroism saved his brother's sight. A scratch ran through the soft skin just under Abe's eye.

"Best not tell Mama," said Paul, who saw how close the talon had been. "She's having the baby, best not tell her."

Abe sat in the dirt, bloody-cheeked and crying. Paul shooed the chickens back away out of the alley and under a house.

"You won't tell Mama will you?" he asked.

"Uh-uh," said Abe, agreeing to his first conspiracy.

"Good," said Paul. "Let's find some candy."

Paul held out his hand to help his brother up. Abe rubbed his unbloodied eye with the back of his hand, then put it out to his brother. His hand felt small and slimy when Paul took it. Paul could feel his brother's twiggy bones, and he wondered about the new baby that was being born.

HARBINGERS

THAT THE BABY SPOKE WAS NEWS ENOUGH and it spread. Bell's mother said nothing, and so it must have been her sons who mentioned it to their playmates. Those playmates told their mothers. Those mothers dismissed the information—*you heard wrong, don't tell tales*—but thought it would not hurt to take something, a pie or some preserved fruit or meat, to welcome the baby. The women cooed at the baby. Bell said "Hello." The women's faces changed: their cheeks hollowed, their eyes narrowed, and they backed away. Bell, swaddled in crocheted blankets and thick cloth diapers, fixed her too-young eyes and watched them.

"Hello?" she said again, plaintive, wondering, her tiny preternatural voice sounding both too old and too young.

Bell's mother, whose name was Frances Allen but was called Ann, sat with the bundle of Bell in her arms in the small rocker in front of the coal hearth in a room full of secondhand furniture and wallpaper peeling at the corners, her brown hair falling loose to her shoulders where it had come undone and she hadn't bothered to fix it. Bell's mother smiled uneasily at the women in the parlor. She was tired and full of worry for her daughter. She worried that this little girl, innocent enough to be different, would suffer for it. She worried that Bell's father had not responded to her letters nor sent any money. She wondered how they were going to eat once the neighborhood ran out of curious women and their cold meat pies. She worried what would happen if the women in the room turned on the child in her arms.

Please, Ann seemed to say to them. *I have loved your strange and terrible children. Love mine.*

"Hello?" Bell said again.

The women, in their handmade dresses with machine-made lace, stayed back. Then Millie Cross, short, slight, and brittle-boned, moved in close to look at the baby girl. Millie wore her hair in long braids wrapped around her head and Ann had once joked to her common-law husband that those braids weighed more than Millie, but her husband had not laughed. Millie Cross came forward. She smiled at Ann. She smiled at Bell, put a skinny crooked finger out for the baby to grab. Bell took it in her stubby pink fist.

Minnie laughed, turned to the other women in the parlor. "Just like any child," she said.

"Hello," said Bell again, and Minnie Cross—still smiling—pulled her finger away.

The other mothers felt they must say something and decided to compliment the child. How precocious. What a lovely voice. What a comfort to have a daughter after two sons, a daughter to help you, a daughter to talk to.

"To talk to," said Bell.

"Yes," said Ann Allen to the wonder in her arms, thinking, *Please do not let this be a ruin for her. Or for us.*

"Yes," said Bell.

To the other mothers she was too terrible, too fat and peach-colored, an infant who could not yet hold up her own head but could focus her eyes on them and say their names. There was some speculation, among a certain set, that the baby was actually much older than Bell's mother claimed. Another theory, from those who'd read in the morning papers of Charles Darwin's cousin Francis Galton and his burgeoning new science of eugenics, was that Bell was some sort of new breed of human, an advanced being, the harbinger of the new race. Others, who read the evening news, found it unlikely that the new breed of human would be begat by such a woman with two unruly boys.

An old widow who had come without bringing anything for the child or her mother announced loudly to the room that no good would come of this, and then let herself out. The other mothers tittered. Ann Allen rocked her baby girl, cooed to her as she would to any child, told her not to worry over what the women had said.

And Bell spoke but said little.

BROTHERS, AGAIN

BELL'S BROTHERS WANTED VERY MUCH to hate the little girl who took all attention away from them.

"Come meet her," said their mother on the day of Bell's birth, without first asking where they had been. This omission riled Abe so much that he had an urge to walk outside without even greeting the baby and to look for something to throw at pigeons.

The baby lay next to their mother. The boys came up to the foot of the bed and peered through the cast iron bars. Their mother held the baby up so they could see her face.

"You can come closer," said their mother.

The baby was fat and piglet-colored, with a short nose and bow-shaped lips.

"We can see from here," said Paul.

"What happened to your face, Abe?" asked his mother with a drowsy sort of concern when she noticed the scratch and the puffiness under his eyes. Abe stayed behind the bars, put his dirty hands up to his face as if he could hide it from her.

"He fell," said Paul.

"Well," said their mother, "come around and meet your sister."

The boys crept closer, around the side of the bed.

"Don't be scared," their mother said. *She is strange, but don't be scared.*

The baby opened her eyes and looked at them.

Had their baby sister been an ordinary baby, she most likely would have suffered the sudden, inexplicable infant death that afflicts so many third children, found blue in their bassinets by mothers who had left them only moments earlier. But she disarmed her older siblings, for even pink and wrinkled she was a lovely baby and even at five and seven they were only little men and later that day when she first said their names, in her clear, bubbly voice, they fell in love with her—for a while.

ANSWERS

WHEN MINNIE CROSS'S OWN DAUGHTER'S second child was born dead, Minnie decided to bring her daughter to see Bell. They came with pickled cabbage, sweet and milky rice, and lemon squares. Ann fetched the baby from the basket in the bedroom.

"Can I?" asked Minnie's daughter, eyes red-rimmed and dark-circled, and she held out her chicken bone arms to take Bell.

"She's stronger than she looks," Minnie reassured.

Ann put the bundled baby into the young woman's arms. Bell smiled and said hello. Minnie's daughter held Bell's face to her own and asked the questions she needed answers to, one after another, about her child, and life before birth and what death is and how Heaven is for babies and could she have the same baby again if she tried. Her breath was thick with tears and the questions tumbled over themselves, too many, too fast.

Paul and Abe stood in the corner and soon became embarrassed, so slunk out the back before it was too late.

"Yes," said Bell to Minnie Cross's weeping daughter. "Yes, and yes, and yes."

After Minnie and her daughter's visit, Bell's mother

began taking in food and payment in return for her daughter's talent, a trade which made her uneasy. Mostly it was nonsense Bell gave out, faint burblings of names and blessings, snatches of rhymes and children's prayers; but when she was thought to have correctly predicted both a train derailment and a large and violent storm, her fame spread. Bell briefly became a minor institution: a small hope to the uncertain and superstitious. Ann Allen took the food and the money, but was wary of a world that would want so much from a child.

When Bell was a few weeks old, the telegraph got as far as Montana and Bell's mother, assuming her previous letters were lost, sent a wire off to her common-law husband reading:

BABY GIRL BORN SPEAKS NAME BELL

A week later, a letter came in response, admonishing the waste of money wiring when postcards were a penny each, and hoping Bell was a nickname for Dorothy and only in a postscript—she speaks soon?—hinting at his fear that the baby was not made by him nine months before her birth but before that, and might not then be his. The father did not mention in the letter the thing that disturbed him most, that on the morning before the telegraph arrived, he woke to see his child, swaddled in the rough camp blankets at the foot of his cot, her sweet pink head shining through. He had reached for her, taken her in his arms, felt her before she disappeared into the folds of gray wool. She was, he thought, much too heavy for an infant, as if she were pulled by some engine, or some weight hung from her, and he thought *I must help her, uncouple her from this burden,* and then she was gone.

He told no one of this visitation, but it slipped in and out of his mind, distracting him just enough that before his letter reached his family, he was killed.

There were a hundred ways a man could die putting in the line—blown to bits, crushed by loose stacked ties, cleaved by wheels, ripped apart by couplings, or flattened or trampled or more. He must have died tragically, brutally, thought Ann, because the rail company sent her money, and the company never would have sent money unless they were trying to cover up something awful. Bell's mother took the money and never asked what happened to him, the legal fact of their never marrying now no issue at all because he was dead and she was accepting his widow's pension.

With the money she decided to stop her infant's fortune-telling trade and to try and raise her as a normal baby girl. Ann Allen told herself she would not question her daughter, that it was wrong, anyway, to know too much about the future or the past. But sometimes, when the baby was sleeping, she would speak aloud her fears, hoping Bell might wake up and tell her something that would make things easier. But Bell never did.

INHERITANCE

PAUL HAD A NAKED LADY. His father gave her to him, just before he'd left again, this time to be a foreman for a team of drivers building the Chicago, Burlington and Quincy Rail. He sat Paul down to have the talk a man has with his oldest son when he is leaving again for a long while, even if the oldest son is only six. Paul's father told him he would have to look after his mother and brother and the new baby when it came and that he was to try to be a faithful and obedient boy, try harder than his old man. He gave Paul a map of the country and showed Paul where he was going, tracing the line across the wide rivers and shaded mountains, up through the pink and blue and orange lands in the West. He told Paul about building the line, and Paul imagined the men pulling rail and ties from his father's carts while a steam engine closed in behind them. Paul's father also gave him for safe keeping a medal his own father—for whom Paul was named—had received for building Lincoln's bridge at Paducah in the Rebels' War. Finally, he gave Paul a small photographic card—a picture of a woman with her hair in curls held by a circlet of silver, smiling slightly at the corners or her mouth and looking off to her right. With her right arm, she leaned heavily on a sword, and with her left she held a set of silver balance scales. Across her neck and flowing behind her she wore a velvety cape, which pooled at her feet, but she wore nothing else. The bottom of the card, in curling type, bore the word *Justice*.

"I thought," said Paul's father, "this one would be best, because it has a sword, and young boys love swords."

The picture made Paul uncomfortable; he squeezed his hands between his thighs and looked away.

Why this? thought Paul.

But his father did not explain.

BUTTER

Bell would stick her finger in the pot of butter, tickling, hooking her finger to the side, scraping out a rich inch. In her mouth it tasted thick and secret. Bell's older brothers gave her butter while their mother wasn't looking. They let her suck it off their fingers, or fed her spoonfuls like pabulum. Bell's mother scolded the boys for indulging her.

"You've never been hungry," she said to them. *It is good for a person to learn their hunger,* thought their mother. *It is good for a person to find the edge.* She worried for her indulged daughter. She worried too that a baby who could speak could turn into a girl who—what?—she worried she didn't know.

"You'll get fat," she said to Bell. "You'll get spots. You'll smell greasy and sour."

Bell ignored her mother. As she grew, into a seemingly normal little girl, she didn't get any fatter than she should be. She never had any more blemishes than usual. Bell spread butter thick on bread, dropped clotted, milky spoonfuls on her cooked carrots, in her porridge. She ate her birthday cake with butter cream frosting, with extra butter. She smelled sweet like shortbread, soft like biscuits, churning like cream.

BLUE

AS A TODDLER, BELL SPOKE TO EVERYTHING. She made the noises of squirrels and seagulls, cats and sparrows, but was content also to speak to them in English. She spoke to the elms and the clover, to the box elders with their buds in spring. She spoke to curbstones, lampposts, trash bins. As she grew older, her babbling made her brothers dislike taking her out in public.

"Hello pig," said Bell one afternoon to the sign on the butcher shop when she and her brothers were on an errand for their mother. "Hello sign," she said to it too.

"Hello stone," she sang out. "How are you, dirt, how are your leaves today, flowers?"

"Hello rail, green, brown, poop," she sang to a railing, the sign for the grocer, and to the dog shit in the street.

"Shut up, Bell," said Abe, who was holding her hand.

Paul said nothing for he was in front leading them somewhere.

"Hello bricks, hello bank, hello blue," said Bell.

Abe grimaced as he led her by a bank branch dressed in a considerable amount of red, white, and blue bunting.

"Hello bank," she said louder, "I love your red I love your white I love your blue, blue.

"RED AND RED AND WHITE AND BLUE," she shouted with glee.

Abe stopped in the street and slapped her hard across the face. Paul was far enough ahead he didn't see. This was the first time anyone had hit Bell. She was startled silent. She did not know what to do but take some cue from Abe—who stood tall in front of the bank and bunting, red and white wings sprouting behind—Abe, who was waiting for something, something awful. And then she remembered the pain, and her burning face, and she let out a long, pitiful cry.

Paul stopped when he heard it. He turned to see Bell, red and swollen and wide mouthed.

"What happened?" Paul asked Abe.

"She fell," said Abe.

"You okay?" Paul asked Bell. She shook her head. "Don't worry," said Paul, "you can ride on my back the rest of the way."

And before Paul leaned down to let Bell scramble up him, he punched Abe hard in the shoulder.

"What'd you do that for?" asked Abe, his eyes welling up with tears that he was determined not to cry, and mad he couldn't hit Paul back now that his brother had his sister on his back. He rubbed his arm, wished his sister who thought so highly of herself had never been born.

Bell hugged tight around Paul's neck and he pulled at her arms so she wouldn't choke him. "Abe," she said. "Abraham Allen, I didn't fall, you know I didn't. Abraham, Abraham Allen."

And Paul, tired, said "Oh, shut up, Bell."

And she did.

SNAKE

ABE FOUND A KNIFE, a little mother of pearl-handled pocketknife, in the stones on the ground outside their house, when he was seven or eight. *Just like King Arthur*, he thought.

The Allen house was built on unsteady land, on timbers driven into the mud. There were fourteen steps up to the first floor, and a large, dirt-bottomed basement where cats and rats and roosters fought for a home in winter. In the dozen feet or so between the steps and the street was a scrubby bit of dirt lawn, where Bell's mother every spring tossed marigold seeds and where every spring and summer marigolds failed to grow but where morning glory and wild fennel came up despite the weeding. And between the scrubby lawn and the broken stone street was a little rut, filled with pebbles, and in the pebbles, Abe found the knife. He decided to hide it from Paul, add it to a collection of his own secret things, like the picture postcard of a naked lady with the sword he'd found under his brother's mattress. Abe thought of all the things the blade was useful for—cutting leather, loosening stuck things from crevices, cutting the tail off a dead rat, defending his turf from rivals, himself from bullies, slicing another boy, giving him scars.

The knife was rusted open and the blade dull, but he oiled it with sewing machine grease and sharpened it with a nail file. Once it was clean, he carried it all the time. He put his hand in his pocket to feel it. He practiced opening it until he could get it with just one hand. The knife made him feel older, gave him secret authority. He touched it in his pocket when he saw strangers and thought *I can hurt you.*

A younger boy crossed the street toward Abe one evening while Abe was counting marbles. He'd taken the marbles out of a drawstring bag his mother made for him, and was arranging them by size and shape and color on the patch of not-so-muddy grass in front of his house. He was not looking for a game. Abe knew the other boy; he vaguely knew all the boys around in the neighborhood, and he did not have a good reason to think that Timmy or Jimmy or Tommy was coming to take something. He had every reason to believe that the boy had seen him, in the public space, with marbles out, and had taken it as an informal invitation to play. Most likely, the boy was going to say *Abe what have you got there?*

But Abe wanted to be left alone.

Lessons must be learned. Someone must take up the mantle, even at a young age, of keeper of the order. To eat is to kill, to take a wage is to steal one from another man, to strike is to load a policeman's pistol. By ten, Abe would have a trick jackknife, a bowie knife with a scabbard, and another for his brother. By eleven, he could have from other boys his own age or even a little older almost anything he'd want—

money, toys, pigeons, candy—just by asking, although he would not ask often. By twelve, when the fire came, his name would be known by adolescent boys even outside his own neighborhood, and girls he didn't know would smile and laugh and whisper to their friends and follow him, and to his satisfaction his fame would outspread even his sister's, the girl who spoke so soon.

Before the boy finished crossing the street, Abe had the knife out of his pocket, unfolded its blade. When the boy arrived, standing over Abe on the ground, Abe raised the knife in his hand and the stained blade reflected the falling sun. Abe stared at the boy and said nothing, just held the knife and stared, meaning *See here? Like Arthur I have pulled sword from stone. This is my Excalibur.* The other boy started crying and ran home.

Abe, a middle child, had come into his power.

STARS

WHEN BELL WAS FOUR, she asked her mother what stars looked like, because she had never seen them in the flat city sky. Ann took her daughter on the City Rail to the farthest stop west. It was Bell's first train; she pressed her face to the glass, fogged it with her breath. They alighted in a neighborhood still partially under construction: houses set far apart, some not yet finished, a boulevard of trees running down the middle. They stood on a tree lawn away from lights, and Ann Allen held her daughter up and pointed to the constellations: the Hunter, the Dragon, the Bears large and small, the North Star.

"Are they always there?" asked Bell.

"Yes," said her mother. "Always."

"Even when we can't see them?"

"Yes," said her mother. "They move, sometimes they fall, but they are always there."

"Where do they fall?"

"I'm not sure. Far away. West, maybe." Ann had not seen stars this clear in years. She shivered, set Bell down. Fingers of smoke rose from the stockyards to the east, the city a sooty smudge against dark blue. As the sky arched west, it grew darker, blacker and the stars seemed not so far. In the city, prices went up, her children got older and needed more. Many nights she stayed up worrying.

To Bell, the sky seemed heavy and uncomfortable, weighted down with the stars' beauty. "What is it like to be a star?" she asked.

"I don't know," said her mother. "The Devil was once a star that fell, they say."

Bell could feel her mother's worry. "And they won't fall on us?" she asked.

"No. Of course not," said Ann.

"It's alright," said Bell, trying to comfort her worried mother. "You don't need to lie."

BOYS

Bell loved boys because boys loved her, and Bell loved love above all else. Bell wasn't beautiful. If she had lived in an age of snapshots and home movies, someone would have noticed and pointed it out to her. Her jaw was not sharp, her cheekbones were not high, her eyes too round and her nose too short. But in movement, in even the tiniest action of, say, quietly watching a spider climb a fence, her nose wrinkled, and her eyes glistened, her skin glowed and even her earlobes seemed to shine and radiate a kind of warmth that settled on men's hearts. And men would comment, men she met when she was out with her brothers, or men that used to come to see her mother, on what a beauty she would be, on how much like both an adult and a child she looked, on the peculiar way she stood, or stared at things, or breathed in through her mouth and out through her nose with a quiet sigh. Boys would put down their sticks or marbles or jacks when she walked by, put down their things and look up to say hello.

THE DEVIL

BELL'S FIRST CRUSH, AT AGE SIX, was a boy about her age named Walter Bell. Walter had a round and cherubic prettiness that delights in youth but would most likely look uncomfortable and rubbery as he aged. Bell loved him. She imagined they would marry; she marched up and down the parlor, pantomiming her dress, her bouquet. Her name would be Bell Bell, and it was the loveliest name she could imagine.

Walter Bell knocked on the door one early evening, saw her brothers were not there, and asked if he could see her naked.

In the back room, Bell's mother navigated a sea of forms, insurance claims, looking for legal remedies to her abandonment and near-poverty. Outside the lamplighter lit the gas lights, one after another, with the flame on a long, trim stick. In the front room, Bell took off her cotton drawers and pulled up her play dress. Walter assessed.

"You're not much, really," said Walter.

"No," said Bell, upset. "I suppose not."

"Bell," called her mother. "Is someone here?"

Walter went pale and nervous. Bell quickly let her dress go.

"Only Walter," said Bell.

"Who?" asked her mother. *Only Walter,* thought Bell. She

had an urge to kick him, but instead she cursed him in her own mind, a curse she knew from fairy stories.

"Only no one," called out Bell to her mother as she opened the door and pushed Walter out. When he was gone, she lit a safety match, pinched it out with her fingertips. Then she lit another. Her brothers came home to their mother asleep on the paper-covered bed, and their sister sitting in the parlor by the coal fire, her undergarment on the rug, half a box of matches burnt around her, singing her own name.

DREAMER

PAUL LIVED THE LIFE OF A PROPHETIC DREAMER, but he did not know it, because he rarely saw the outcomes of his dreams. Once, he dreamt of a young girl losing grip on her mother's hand in the torrent tide of a bloody river but had no way of knowing that somewhere in Tennessee a creek rose faster than could be escaped and though the girl never drowned, the mother did. He saw an airship pull from its tether of a thousand disembodied hands and float off into the darkness of space like a toy balloon, but did not know that halfway around the world a crowd of Parisians watched in horror as the same ship crashed into a children's school at recess. Or that the man in the red jacket who chased him through the night with a pride of lions and a rifle that was also a sword was the same man who, with a pack of golden hunting dogs, tracked down errant diamond miners in Rhodesia. Had he lived longer, into the full bloom of "news" and "wires," when the ubiquity of the film camera and half-tone teletype prints let pictures, images, and events swim seas and fly across the open spaces of the world, he might have come to see how his dreams were cut from the cloth of the actual happenings of the world, not from his personal psyche. He would have opened newspapers to pictures of his own dreams, to conflagrations and petty violences all over the globe. Instead, he lived in a time where the news was just learning to be new, and his dreams were simply his.

One night when Paul was seventeen or eighteen, he dreamt of a giant bell, and within it a small bell, and within that another smaller bell, one inside the other like nesting dolls. In front of him a cord to pull, but the bell would make no sound, for it had no clapper, no tongue. Instead, as he pulled it, the giant bell full of bells shot towards him and he crouched as the bells fell and he woke up on the davenport in the parlor of his mother's house, his sister asleep in the next room at the foot of his mother's bed.

Twenty years before his dream, in Germany, Emperor Wilhelm had given twenty-two captured French cannons for the making of the Kaiserglocke, the largest bell of all time, which could only be cast in a giant pit dug in the ground. Two times it could not be tuned, and so it had to be melted down and cast again. French prisoners of war heated the bell metal in giant crucibles over oil flame until the metal became oily itself. The bell maker shouted a count for the simultaneous tipping of the molten bronze into the channels of the mold. Soldiers knew how to keep time. Nearly twenty years after Paul dreamed of the bell, the Kaiser's grandson would reverse the process, have the giant bell melted down and turned into Krupp's Howitzers, Big Berthas, the largest guns the world had ever seen.

Paul did not know of the Kaiserglocke, did not know the bell in his dream foretold spasms of the next century, the destruction of Europe, the deaths of millions of young men. He thought the bell that might explode and crush him slept in the next room. He had promised his mother, whatever happened to her, he would watch his sister, keep her safe. He did not know his prophetic power had little to say about him.

And what use would prophecy have anyway, except in hindsight, except to know you saw something, a glimpse of the invisible wonder that connects the things of the world, the mechanism in shadow, its movement perfect and unstoppable? It would not help Paul, anyway, to know the meanings of his dreams.

SLEEP

BELL DID NOT DREAM. Her brothers and her mother described dreaming to her and she could not understand it. Bell fell asleep into blackness and woke up into the world and nothing happened in between.

BURN

WHEN BELL WAS SEVEN, a fire swept through their neighborhood on the west side of the city on the lake. It was a hot dry summer and someone lit a match to, or an ember fell on, or a cigar got tossed in, a rubbish pile: a fermenting, hissing pile full of the combustible gases made by rotting horses and chicken guts and pulp paper and shit and bits and pieces.

It was not a big fire, not in the history of a city known for burning, but Bell's house was destroyed, along with half a dozen other buildings on the street, and a litter of puppies was killed. All of her things were destroyed, and things she'd found that were not hers too—the only known photograph of her father, with his drooping, unfashionable mustache; the medal her grandfather got in the war; the French postcard of naked Justice—and all of the secret things that her mother had managed to keep hidden even from a curious daughter like Bell. No people died in the blaze, but the fire burnt her mother, who was napping, badly on one arm and in her insides, nearly killing her. The fire gave her six years of fits, sending up each lung a teaspoonful at a time.

Bell and her brothers were out of the neighborhood,

down by the lake. They'd walked down, out on the rocks in the water by the jetty. Bell's brothers, fourteen and twelve, had their shirts off, their pant legs rolled up, and were showing off for the neighborhood girls who'd followed them down. Bell kicked off her boots and jumped into the water in her play dress, a thin, striped cotton sheath with a dark pinafore. She emerged cocooned, material stuck to her thin legs. Her dress turned translucent while her brothers talked to girls in corsets, in pale calicos. Bell stood wet in her little girl dress, pulling material away from her skin, which plastered itself back as soon as she let it go as if sucked by a vacuum tube.

"I'm wet," she said, to nobody in particular and everyone around her.

"Paul, I'm wet," she said to Paul.

"Abe, I'm wet," she said to Abe.

Abe called back, "Bell, we can see you're wet, you don't have to go on about it."

"I'm not drying," said Bell.

"Well, run around," said Paul. Bell considered this, wrung out her skirt as best she could, gathered it in handfuls at her hips, and ran the length of the jetty, back and forth.

"Let your skirt go, it will dry faster," said Paul.

"Take off your pinafore and lay it on the stones," said one of the calico girls. Bell ran over to Paul to be unbuttoned and she held down her sheath dress while he pulled off the pinafore and then she resumed her running. The air over the city rippled with heat and smut. Far from the lake a fire bell rang and the smoke of Bell's burning house mixed with the smoke of the factories and breweries and slaughterhouses and ships and trains and burning rubbish.

"I'm drying," she called back to them as she ran. Her bare feet slapped warm stone. With each lap, the cotton clung to her less, became more opaque, the outlines of her nipples and her bloomers disappeared. The boys talked to the girls, the cuffs of their pants heavy and wet, the girls sweating at the smalls of their backs and through the material at their armpits, the girls taking their boots off, pulling their stockings down, dipping their toes into the water.

"Look, I'm drying," called Bell as they ignored her flying back and forth across the jetty, unaware.

"Look," she said. "I'm almost dry."

BLOOD

THE AFTERNOON OF THE FIRE they returned from the lake
and found the house burned down and their mother taken
to the hospital. In place of their house stood a dark wet
pile, and near it a water wagon, pulled by a team of horses
still lathered from the journey over. The house was gone
in minutes, said the water wagon man.

Paul asked after his mother and Abe asked about the fire,
the destruction.

Bell climbed towards the house over overturned buckets,
thinking of her things: her dolls and her stories and her
clothes and her drawings, burnt and buried. She wanted to
collect the ashes of it all, save the remains, but the rubble
was still too hot to go near. Instead, she sat on the stoop
of an untouched two-flat across the way, holding onto her
knees, and watching her brothers and the firemen talk.
Then she heard a small sad sound. She followed it, down
around the burnt block, making her way down the alley,
listening. Behind the burnt block, a little outbuilding,
a garden shed, had caught fire, and its roof had fallen in
between its walls. In the alley stood a whimpering, frantic
dog—a yellow mutt with hanging teats. Her fur was singed
about the face. She pawed at the wreck of the outbuilding

through the doorframe, pushed her nose between the boards. Bell watched, unsure what to do. The dog made slow passage through the timbers into the remains of the building and disappeared.

Bell heard her brothers calling for her.

Bell called back. "I'm here," she said. "I'm here, but I can't come just now." Paul and Abe came down the alley, pants still wet at the hems.

"We've got to go," said Paul. "We've got to go now."

"Look," said Bell.

The mama dog came out with a puppy in her mouth, a puppy scorched black, and pink where the black cracked, with no eyes, a puppy like a cooked rabbit and the dog laid the puppy down at Bell's feet and began to lick it, the big mama tongue covering the whole puppy's body, and she licked and licked it until she had eaten the whole thing up.

"I'm sorry," Bell said to the dog. "I have to go. I'm sorry."

The Allen children felt so dirty when they got to the hospital, like soot on clean cotton, graphite smudged across a page.

They spoke to the pointed hat nurses in black and white gowns who shushed them and went back to floating in and out of green curtains. Finally, a narrow-faced woman asked them their names and told them to wash their hands with large chalky bars of disinfecting soap before they went and saw their mother behind a curtain near the end.

Bell could not help but run and climb onto her mother, hug her.

"Careful," said her bandaged mother as Bell tried to

arrange herself on the little hospital cot and wrap her arms across her mother's chest. Her mother could not put her arms around the child, but leaned and kissed her cheek.

"I'm fine," their mother said.

Paul and Abe stood at the foot of the bed, Paul looking older, his mother thought, than when she'd seen him that morning. The dirt and smoke had chiseled him, had grown him. Not Abe, Ann thought, nor Bell, her baby, warm and soft and safe next to her.

"If I died," asked Bell, "would you eat me?"

"No," said her mother, shocked. "No, of course not. No, that's horrible."

"Oh," said Bell. "I thought maybe, but I guess I was wrong."

"She saw a dog eat its dead puppy," said Abe.

Bell slid off the bed and turned from their mother, crying. Paul came and put his arm around her.

"Bell, you have to be careful, we are in a hospital," Paul whispered. "You need to bite your tongue."

Bell put her tongue between her teeth and bit softly, then hard enough to punish, to make it bleed. It felt as if the world were changing too quick, but her teeth on her tongue kept her steady. A thin-faced nurse swanned down the corridor and asked the children please to not touch anything or to get on the bed because they had already gotten the sheets dirty and that a burn might easily become infected or worse.

Bell kept her mouth closed the rest of the time they were with their mother in the hospital that day, so that no one could see the blood.

WORDS

BELL LOVED WORDS.

She read everything she could find, everything her brothers would bring her: dime stories, papers in the morning and the evening. She read Frank R. Stockton's "The Lady or the Tiger?" and *The Hundredth Man* and Frances Hodgson Burnett's *That Lass O'Lowrie's* and *Little Lord Fauntleroy*. She read Andrew Lang's *Fairy Books* both *Red* and *Blue*. She saw herself in a hundred different peasant daughters, princesses, millers, and miners; she saw herself especially in the boys and girls who are delivered one day a forgotten inheritance, a secret from their infancy, saved from ancient injustice which unbalanced their worlds. Stories made the world make sense to her, and she read aloud to herself, listening to the words, marveling at the strangeness of the way the characters spoke.

Bell loved the sounds of words: how her own name hit and chimed; how *star* sparkled, all angles, and *smoke* lifted and vanished. Even more, she loved the feel of the language in her mouth; buzzing v's and z's, explosive b's and p's, the moist final l's of her own name. She stood at the mirror in the parlor and watched her mouth make words, lips and tongue arching, bowing, flicking. It filled her up, watching herself, as she was just coming into her own, full of hum and tremble, just ready to ring.

JUSTICE

WHEN THE WORLD'S COLUMBIAN EXPOSITION came in 1893, Paul and Abe went first to the Montana Exhibition because Montana was where their father had died. The plaster palace displayed a thousand artifacts of Montaniana: taxidermied bison, a Blackfoot feathered crown, a forty-pound copper nugget, and, in sapphires, rubies, and quartz shards, a glittering mosaic of the American flag. In the middle of the hall stood a clothed Justice, solid silver in a glass case, her dress streaming behind her as if caught by wind, her feet barely touching ground, and Paul thought *there she is with her scales* and Abe thought *there she is with her sword.*

With the insurance from the fire, their mother had found her family a nicer, if smaller, house. But, soon after the Exposition, the railroad company went bust, their mother lost her pension, and the boys quit school. Abe was already working as a sometime messenger, collector, corner watcher for the local boys. Paul delivered groceries after school. It was a moment, Paul later reflected, where they might have done things differently, left the city perhaps, gone west themselves, but Abe kept on collecting and watching, working for bookies and loan makers, carrying knives and worse, and Paul went from delivery boy to cart loader at a grocers' supply to apprentice teamster. He left early in the mornings and as he walked to the stables behind the grocers' warehouse near his house, as he passed through the smell of a hundred thousand pigs penned for slaughter wafting up from the south, he sometimes thought of his father overseeing teams of horse carts in mysterious, treasure-filled, deadly Montana. He thought of his father as he teamed his pair, bridled and collared them, slipped the leather blinders over their dark and cautious eyes.

The horses themselves smelled of the pigs' deaths. Were they inured to the scent of their captive countrymen from the land of animals, Paul wondered, and ignorant to their own similar fate? He led the horses out to work. It is a pensive thing to spend your time around dumb animals. He thought of the pigs, of bacon, of slaughterhouse workers. He thought of rail lines that brought the pigs and of silver. Of the men who had financed the Chicago, Burlington and Quincy, who had let it fail, had let his father die. How much of the invisible smell of death was on them?

On the street, the horses' clomping footfalls woke up the drunks passed out against the walls of the tavern on the corner.

"Get," called Paul as the drunks scrambled out of the way of the cart. "Get."

FAIR

ABE AND PAUL BROUGHT A TINTYPE HOME they'd had made at the Turkish Exposition at the Fair; in it they wore heavy turbans and long robes, lay on carpet-covered benches and held long, metallic pipes.

"You're real Princes of Araby," said their mother, who put the photograph in its paper frame on the table by her bed.

They told Bell and their mother about Montana, about the Midway and the moving walkway by the grand Casino, about the German armaments exposition with a twenty-two-foot Krupp gun. Their mother asked about the self-heating irons and instant breakfasts, but the boys had not seen those; they told her instead about fruit-flavored chewing gum. They did not tell their mother and sister about how they spent too much money seeing the Egyptian hootchie-kootchie dancers in translucent silk pajamas and fringed veils, or about how Abe and his friends wanted to set up games outside the Midway, away from the guards, or about how Paul wanted to go back to hear the beautiful Florence Kelley speak about factories and fair wages. He would go, and find the mannish Jane Addams instead. Still, he would stay and he would listen.

"Will you take me?" asked Bell.

She wanted to be a Princess of Araby. She wanted to ride the gondolas on the lagoon, and the Ferris wheel at night with its electric lights turning up into the sky. She wanted to see the people from all over: the caged pygmies, the feathered Indians, the pale Japanese ladies in wooden sandals, the tall Vikings and their wooden ships, and Buffalo Bill and Annie Oakley and the Wild West Show. Bell loved the whole world and it felt so close, only a mile away or so. If only she could get there.

"Of course," said her brothers.

Of course they would, they said, take their sister to the White City, grown gray from smoke and fumes, full of a thousand hucksters, tricksters, and scams, and a thousand lines to see a thousand thousand paintings and artifacts and things, taxidermied animals and preposterous machines, which blended together in an electrified glow and whirl especially dangerous to young girls, so easily seduced as they were by novelty candies and celluloid trinkets into bright, hidden rooms smelling of chloroform, where they would be violated by foreigners, exposed by men with flash powder and dry-plate cameras—so quick!—their images for sale in the back of souvenir shops to those who knew to ask, or so all the newspapers warned.

Of course they would take her, they said, because they had never learned how to say no to her. She waited and imagined—what?—that there was a world where she would be recognized, that the Fair was the place where someone, Annie Oakley, a Viking, would find her and say *Here you are, the one we wanted, the magical baby now a magical girl.* She knew the route and where her mother kept her cash, and she imagined going but she was afraid to go on her own.

And then the Fair was over and Annie Oakley and the Vikings had gone and her brothers never took her and the papier-mâché palaces were ruined by rain and no one had found her and no one would.

STORIES

WHEN BELL WAS TEN OR ELEVEN, and living in a new house in a different part of the city, her schoolmates discovered that she had been the girl who spoke too soon and punished her for it.

Two different Marys told her that their mothers had forbade them from playing with her, and square-faced Helen Green's mother had said to be sure not to touch anything Bell had touched. A teacher told Helen not to tell stories when she overheard her in the yard recounting Bell's strangeness—how Bell spoke even coming out of her mother, how she could talk to ghosts and angels and the devil and could tell your fortune like a gypsy. Bell said it isn't a story, and the teacher told Bell not to lie either, not to embellish.

When the teacher walked away, Bell said to the girls "It's true"—and tall, athletic Helen stomped across the paved lot to tell the teacher that Bell was embellishing some more.

"I'm not lying," Bell called after Helen, and Helen's friend Barbara with the tiny eyes pinched Bell's arm, twisted the skin and said, "You heard, Bell, don't lie."

Bell rubbed her arm, watched the twisted skin bloom into the outline of a kiss. "I didn't lie," she said.

"You think you're something special," said beady-eyed Barbara, wielding the phrase like a pocket knife, testing its power. "You think you're something special, but you're not."

Bell thought, *but it's true*; yet even she began to wonder what was true. She did not remember, she knew only what her brothers and mother told her when she was little, which they never talked about any more. It's true, she told herself again. And Barbara was right. She did think herself extraordinary. She felt herself full with something unknowable, a power, a magic that might burst from her fingers at the merest touch.

Bell touched Barbara's arm to show her. Barbara swatted it away.

It's true. I think I'm special but I'm not, thought Bell and bit her tongue, tasted her salt and blood. When Helen and the teacher returned, Bell was sobbing, and when the teacher asked what happened Bell opened her bloody mouth and Helen and Barbara screamed and the teacher sent Bell home, telling her not to come back again.

BLESSING

WHEN BELL WAS NEARLY FOURTEEN her mother took to bed to die. The fire-brought consumption claimed her. She went to bed three months before her end and Bell tended her, bathed her, washed her bloody handkerchiefs and emptied the bed pan, rubbed camphor on her chest. At first Bell's mother ballooned in the bed, her ankles swelling up to the size of butcher's hams, and then she shrank again, shriveled and pruned, skin flaking and joints raw.

Bell took care of her mother as best she could.

"How do I face this death without a blessing or a gift?" Bell's mother asked on a day she thought might be the end. "You have one, Bell. You have one, but I have nothing." Ann turned her face away, hid the bits she coughed into a handkerchief. Bell sat on a small chair near the bed and said nothing.

"I don't know how to do this, Bell," her mother said, crumbling into her bed sheets. Bell did not know either. She wanted someone to tell her the magic words to say. She invented as she went along, making watery soups and pungent teas. She read to her mother, slept next to her to keep her warm. She wondered whether from the beginning, everything had been leading her like a train upon rails to a place where she met her own uselessness.

The neighborhood knew the woman was dying, and knew that her sons had abandoned her to death as much as they could. It was Bell who stayed with her. The girl. *How lucky you are to have a daughter*, said the neighbors, *a daughter to take care of you.*

A doctor came and said the cause of her dying was drowning, her body filling with water, summoning up a sea inside her, and there was nothing to be done.

"Give your mother some of this," he said, handing Bell a brown bottle of narcotic syrup. "For pain. It will help her sleep."

Bell tasted the medicine when the doctor left, before she gave it to her mother. It tasted of bile, the sugar barely covering the bitter and ill.

REMEDY

BELL WANTED SO MUCH.

Bell had seen the advertisements in magazines, pictures of girls her own age in steel busked training corsets—"Stronger, More Comfortable than Whalebone!"—which promised a 15-inch waist with just one year of continuous wear. She'd seen the fashion plates with their wasp-waists, the New Shape, which thrust the chest forward and the rear back, which bent and molded the body and held it in place with steel and rivets.

No one corseted Bell. She imagined the sharp boning, the tightness, her floating ribs bending down around her viscera, the metal and canvas enclosing her. She imagined it would keep the things from spilling out, the words, the breath, the blood before it reached her tongue. She tied a wide belt around her waist, buckled it tight, pricked her fingers with a needle to help with the pain.

It was one of the many things she wanted: friends, new and lovely clothes; she wanted her mother to not be sick and she wanted her mother to die; she wanted her brother Paul to stay and her brother Abe to leave, her brother Paul to leave and take her with him, to leave on her own; she wanted to discover her father was alive and rich and for him to take her on a train with velvet seats and china dishes, somewhere, anywhere, west. She wanted a boy too, that she'd seen in the papers, a teenaged outlaw who looked to her like an escape.

Most of all she wanted armor she might fold herself into, something to protect her soft insides.

THE BOXER

IN THE DARK STILL ROOM, caring for her mother, Bell thought about dying. She had almost no friends, and she didn't talk to anyone about dying. Watching her mother sleep and wheeze and slosh, she thought of death as a man who will come and offer something in order to get something in return. A diplomat, a negotiator.

While waiting for death, she found in the newspapers a young man named Billy Starr. He was 18. Very fair. Hollow cheeks which cut into a face all angles, with wide-set eyes and a protruding nose. Even in black and white his skin seemed young. He smiled a half smile. A mustache, fair and sparse, grew over his lip and his hair curled a half an inch below his ears. He looked—Bell couldn't put her finger on it—wicked, perhaps? Knowing? Something about his smile, his eyes, his skin. All the other people whose pictures she'd ever seen printed in the paper seemed worn and unformed in comparison; their eyes distant, blurred, their skin sallow and tough, as if they'd been poorly taxidermied, or were wax figures left in the sun. Bell thought Billy looked good in a way that was bad.

She found other pictures in other papers and she cut them out along with articles about the boy's exploits. Billy and his friends robbed banks in Colorado and paymasters in Wyoming. They gave money to widows and orphans, were held as heroes in the mountains where they hid. Billy had twice been arrested and twice escaped; he once had been in the hangman's noose and his boys rescued him at the last. He left notes for the papers to publish, and though they feigned outrage, they published them anyway.

Bell would collect pictures, glue them to cards. She put lace and ribbon around them. She kept articles about him in a little box in the parlor with his picture on top. Her brothers hated this but said nothing.

The day she found Billy, her mother slept, breathing thick and slurpy breaths. Bell woke her mother and asked her what she thought of the boy in the picture.

Her mother took a long, thin breath and replied, "Not much."

"Does he look like someone I know?"

"I don't know everyone you know," said her mother.

"I can't figure. He looks familiar." Bell flattened the photograph against her lap.

Bell's mother saw the confusion that overtook Bell, and recognized it as nothing more than love. Bell had a crush on a photograph. As a girl, Bell's mother had had a crush on a famous featherweight Irish boxer only from seeing a fight bill with a photo plate posted outside an auditorium. The half-naked man in the photograph, all muscled and golden but with sad eyes and an exotic, drooping moustache, made her mother brazen. She had been fourteen, and the evening of the

236 MARGARET PATTON CHAPMAN

advertised fight she waited by the auditorium door, hoping to see him, to touch him, to tell him she loved him. When he arrived in a gray wool suit and hat, and not shirtless in satin short pants, she barely recognized him. He was through the first of the auditorium's double doors before she realized her foolishness and rushed after him, holding out her arm, calling him as if he were a streetcar that might be stopped.

The boxer was named Davey. He was twice her age, and quite small in person, with dark hair and gold skin. Panicked that she might never see him again, she caught his arm in the second doorway, but could say nothing, not even I love you or hello or good luck. Davey stopped and as the men around Davey went to pull her away from him, he took her hand and kissed it on the knuckles, looking her in the eye. Then the men pulled her back and the boxer went into the auditorium and eventually into the purpose-built ring where he lost to his opponent in seventeen rounds in a fight many would later claim was fixed.

Bell's mother went to the station the next day to see him off and he never looked at her even though she waved and called out her undying love. She watched the train disappear and still she waved, still she shouted Davey, it's me, I love you, remember, in a crowd of other girls who called out, some for Davey, some for anonymous young men leaving them behind.

Ann didn't tell Bell about Davey. Instead, she took her medicine when Bell poured it out in brimming spoonfuls, swallowed it hard, and grew yellow in the yellowing room full of sleep.

KISSING

BELL WATCHED HERSELF SAY HIS NAME again and again in the parlor mirror. Billy, William, William Starr. His name looked like a kiss. She imagined finding him, somewhere, finding and then being kissed by him and him taking her away.

Once, she kissed his newsprint photograph, trimmed in ribbon. It tasted of carbon and rag, and where her lips touched it, the ink lifted, the paper pilled, and his face faded away.

GRAVE-DIGGER

IN THE CITY BY THE LAKE, a man did not need a watch. Bells rang at St Aldabert, St Procopius, and St Helen of the Tears, at Holy Cross, Holy Blood, and Holy Trinity, and a hundred more; at the breweries and warehouses and stockyard, a dozen whistles blew. And yet Paul Allen had a watch, a silver switchman's watch, stem-wound, with seventeen-jewel movement and *Crescent St, Waltham, Mass* engraved on the case. Abe gave it to him. Paul knew better than to ask Abe how he came by such a thing.

"You like it?" asked Abe.

Paul liked the watch very much—the feel of it in his hand, the weight in his pocket. He liked its sound, its precision and determination, how it willed itself into the future and him with it.

Paul was twenty, heading into the Trade and Labor Hall to see if there was something better for him who was harnessed by a promise to his dying mother and his sister to whom everyone knew no good would come. Elsewhere in the city, his brother took money to help men, to help them gamble, to help them pay debts, to help them whore. In the hall, a tall Germanic woman with a small head and round glasses called for action, for the rise of an international socialism, for equality of labor and an eight-hour work day, spittle arching over the footlights as she spoke. This was the future. The German woman finished her speech and Paul bought a copy of the weekly *Workmen's Advocate*. Above the masthead ran the words "What the Bourgeoisie Produces, Above All, Are Its Own Grave-Diggers." He folded the paper, put it inside his coat for later, and headed home, the quote rolling around in his mind while he turned the watch stem in his pocket, changing as he walked through the cold, gas-lit night:

What the City Produces, Above All, Are Its Own Grave-Diggers. What Parents Produce, Above All, Are Their Own Grave-Diggers. What Time Produces, Above All, Are Grave-Diggers, Grave-Diggers, Grave-Diggers.

Though his dreams would never tell him, Paul's revolution will never come. His end will come, without justice, in an accident, far too young.

HUSH

ON HIS FINAL VISIT HOME, Abe left the girl he was delivering in the parlor, and went to the bedroom to check on his mother and sister. He was eighteen and taking the girl from one place to another for a friend. It was the middle of the night. He marveled at how soundly his sister and mother slept, how easily anyone could have entered the house, and he resolved to put someone on watch. It was the least he could do.

He watched Bell struggle briefly against her nightshirt, then turn and drape her arm across their shrunken mother. The girl he'd brought called his name softly from the front room and Abe bristled, thinking *quiet, you dumb cunt,* and then *dumb means quiet and stupid, cunt too for that matter.* Thoughts of the dumb bodies on the bed, of the precious and unprotected cunts of his mother and sister, raised a red blade of anger in him, which might only be exorcised against the girl in the other room, and not even against her either because he had promised someone he would get her somewhere, and safely.

Abe knew the edge of his emptiness, and he knew it was sharp and serrated and wide. It drove him, and he was not afraid, unlike his brother who wallowed in shallow sadnesses. Abe was not afraid of anything.

Except his mother was dying, and there was nothing he could do, so he gathered the stupid girl from the front room and left.

CONSEQUENCES

Paul came home late with the evening papers.

"I think it will be soon," said Bell. Ann Allen had shrunk to almost nothing. Bell remembered when her mother seemed the largest, strongest person in the world.

"I should try to find Abe for her," said Paul. They stood quiet for a while on the stoop in the cool air. Paul smoked, kept the newspaper folded under his arm, and the sky shone purple and orange in the lamplight.

"When this is over, can we leave?" Bell finally asked.

"And go where?"

"Somewhere west, don't you think?" said Bell.

Paul saw Bell. She needed new clothes, was too old to wear her little girl smocks anymore, which were stained and ragged. There was so much to do now and more to do after.

"No," said Paul, "we can't." And he stamped out his cigarette. "You get your head so full of ideas."

"You do too," said Bell.

"Maybe," said Paul. He could not imagine that Bell could possibly understand the difference, the weight and worry of the things his head was full of, the size of their import. Not fanciful, not girlish, not like the frivolity of her cares.

"That boy whose picture you cut out has died," Paul said, handing her his paper.

Below the fold, in lithographic relief, was a picture of the shot-up body of her outlaw. Once she'd seen it, Paul wished he'd kept the paper hidden from her. She folded it again neatly in half and handed it back to him.

"Someone should try and find Abe," she said, and she went inside.

ENDS

PAUL WENT TO LOOK FOR ABE in the sorts of places Bell couldn't go and so she was left alone. She gave her mother as much of the medicine as she could swallow, sat by the bed, held her papery hand. Her mother called out and Bell thought, *This is it, this is the end, and here we are, only the two of us.*

"Bell," whispered her mother, but Bell was right there.

The room smelled of the sweetness of the dying, the smell between honey and vinegar.

"Bell," said her mother. "Help."

"I'm sorry," Bell said.

Bell tried her hardest to remember something, something that would help, something from her time as wonder, as oracle—a piece of mystery that could save or comfort her mother. She tried to find words for a gift, words for a blessing, words for a curse. She could not find them. She had once been the baby who spoke, but what good did it do her?

She said nothing. Instead, she lay her head on her mother's chest, listened to the heart dying in the body from which she came. There she waited, for a while.

BARGAIN

WHEN HER MOTHER WAS DEAD and no one seemed to be coming for her, Bell went to the front room and got her box of things.

She took the first article she'd saved about Billy and wrote her name on his name where she found it, in her childish looping pen, tracing her B on top of his, her l's on his, circling the dot of his i with the encompassing eye of her e. Over and over she did this until the pen soaked the newsprint, the nib cut through, covered her hands and dress in ink. She folded the paper smaller and smaller until it was the size of a pill. Some remedy.

She ate it.

The paper was gummy and hard, and when she swallowed she felt it travel the slow line of her throat, sticking, making her gag until she fell on hands and knees to the floor coughing and then it was gone, disappeared within her, as magic.

When it was done, she thought *I tried. I tried, didn't I?* Stars fell, rained on the western places of the world, but to Bell it seemed nothing changed. She had wanted magic, a miracle, some spectacular exchange. She could not recognize that she had planted within herself the seed of becoming, or that the bargain she had made was for a new Bell.

So, covered with ink, she crawled back into bed with her mother's body.

And she didn't speak again for years.

BEGINNINGS, AGAIN

BELL LOVES THE LANDSCAPE. She loves the blur of gold, her breath upon the glass of the train car, the farness and the nearness of the world on the other side. She loves the ghost reflection of herself that appears once the sun sets; her sly companion, floating along beside. She loves the strangers on the car who smile but leave her to herself. She has the last of her mother's money in cash, tucked down in between the stays of her new corset. She has her new wariness there, too.

Paul had come home without Abe to find Bell mute and inky. Later, they buried their mother in a cemetery to the west of the city, carved from prairie land, under open sky. Paul had said it must be like Montana. He had asked Bell what she thought and she did not reply.

Bell will find her way. She is going west where she will seek out the secret places where stars fall and become devils. She will find her way with her new strangeness, her silence. It will be her shield and armor. She has eaten her desire, and it will be her magic charm.

ABOUT THE AUTHOR

MARGARET PATTON CHAPMAN received her MFA from The School of the Art Institute of Chicago. Her short fiction has appeared in *Wigleaf, The Collagist, SmokeLong, Elimae,* and in the anthology *The Way We Sleep,* among others. She is prose editor for *decomP* magazine, and currently lives in Durham, North Carolina.

5 | CHRIS BOWER

A Truth Deeper Than the Truth:
Creating a Full Narrative from Fragments

The Family Dogs

A TRUTH DEEPER THAN THE TRUTH:
CREATING A FULL NARRATIVE FROM FRAGMENTS

When I was 8 years old
while chewing
watermelon-flavored gum
I chased 1 mother rabbit
and 8 baby rabbits
to their deaths.

The mother died
because I chased her
into the street
where she was run over
by a red mini-van
driven by a man
chewing a soon to be discontinued
apple-mango-flavored gum.

He stopped the mini-van
chewed a little slower
on his soon to be discontinued
apple-mango-flavored gum
and stared at me

as I swallowed my watermelon-flavored gum.
Not knowing what to say
I unwrapped another piece of
watermelon-flavored gum
popped it in my mouth
and started chewing
as the red mini-van drove away
with blood spinning off a wheel.

I removed the baby rabbits
one by one
from the rabbit hole
and they quickly escaped my hands
and started running
one by one
to their flattened mother
one by one
into the street and into the wheels
of a blue mini-van
driven by a woman
who was chewing
sugar-free spearmint-flavored gum.

She stopped the blue mini-van
chewed a little slower
on her sugar-free spearmint-flavored gum
and stared at me
as I swallowed my watermelon-flavored gum

254   CHRIS BOWER

and yelled, "Why didn't you stop?"
and she said calmly
between chews
"You shouldn't swallow your gum
It's really bad for you."

EVERYTHING STARTS AS A POEM FOR ME. Going back to when I was a freshman in college, I have written everything— be it an essay, a play, a short story, or a poem—with line breaks and in stanzas.

This means of composition wasn't exactly a choice and the story of how it came about is so stupid, it probably sounds made up. I was using a broken computer with a flawed word processing program that would only allow me to type halfway across the page before it wrapped over to the next line. A lot of my line breaks were just me hitting return before the line jumped down. It became a game to say as much as I could with each line, and everything would fall into a natural rhythm with each line standing on its own as an image or a statement.

I wasn't trying to write poetry, but being mechanically forced to do so taught me a lot about the fragility of language, how to avoid filler, and how to get to the heart of each thought. If each line wasn't doing something other than moving things along, I felt like I was failing, even if I was writing a paper about meth addiction or an essay about Yeats or a story about a boy who had a second set of eyeballs in the back of his knees. On a macro level, my papers, stories, poems, and so forth were sometimes terrible, probably because I was bullshitting my way through the material, but the language, on a micro level, was always very precise and it wasn't until I committed to caring about things as a whole that my writing became something hopefully worth reading. It's great to have interesting lines and moments, but if they don't add up to anything, then what is the point?

For me, poetry has always been where you can really get the essence of language, where you can linger between thoughts, moments, and images and bathe in their connections. Poetry is the most complex and beautiful form of writing, but because I am not usually interested in or capable of being that complicated or beautiful, my work almost never stays in lines and stanzas anymore.

That being said, I don't concern myself with form as much as a lot of writers. I don't sit down and say to myself that I am going to write a poem or a play or a story or a novella. Form and structure are things that I consider after a lot of the material is already written. I take out the line breaks, add punctuation, convert lines into dialogue, turn exposition into narration, and in the process, the form usually reveals itself. I want to be clear that this is not an ideal way to work. It takes me much longer to find my way and often I find the piece is failing, so I go back to the original work and start all over again. The excitement of writing for me is the discoveries I make in the process and the way that stories and characters dictate the form. I ask myself: What else needs to be said? What else needs to happen?

Perhaps unsurprisingly then, *The Family Dogs* did not begin as a novella-in-flash and only found its way to the current form after years of trying it many other ways. I started by writing little poems about a family much like the one I grew up around. My family, like a lot of families, has anecdotes attached to each of us as characters; tiny and fast stories that everyone knows and everyone can tell. While often funny, they are never just jokes and they are often untrue. Events get combined, jumbled, and pasted together until they stick, until the lines are just right. It's all about the stories and while usually in good fun, they often infuriate and humiliate their subjects, but fighting the tales only gives them more power. What these family stories do well is reveal something important about how the person is remembered as a character—as someone from the past: who they used to be, not necessarily a reflection of how they are now. In my family, these types of stories do what fiction is supposed to do: reveal a deeper truth than the truth.

These familial anecdotes evolve but they never disappear and generally find their way into family conversations. It will start with a, "Do you remember when Chris tried to save those rabbits?" then someone will ask, "You mean when he killed those rabbits?" And someone else will pick up from there and finish the story and everyone in the family, except me, will be very happy. In my family, my mother will forever be putting my infant brother on top of the car, only to watch him slide off into a snow bank. My cousin will always be the one that drove his car down the Skokie Swift El tracks in the middle of the night. My great aunt will always have large dogs that looked like deer and ate ice cream sandwiches in single bites. My father will forever be saving my brother from a river vortex, and I will forever be failing to prevent a large amount of baby rabbits from being run over by a minivan. I can do my best to explain my side, but it's a futile gesture. The catastrophic story of rabbit murder might not be the truest story, but it's the one that sticks.

The Family Dogs' main narrator Al is the one who gets to tell his own tiny stories without the rest of the family's interjections and objections. While I wrote nearly a 100 of these stories, the end result was overwhelming and the larger the work became, the more unsatisfying the stories were individually. I found myself, as a storyteller, doing what a novelist might do while developing a short story into a novel, growing minor characters into complete ones. Al, in *The Family Dogs*, would never be interested in doing that, and I allowed the character to guide the form of the work. Had I decided that I wanted to write a novel with these characters, another character would have to tell this story or all the characters would have to speak and tell their versions of events. In the end, I decided that this story was best told with only two different voices and points of view. The individual vignettes became stand-alone flash pieces that all worked together, and I discovered that the form this family story had found was a novella-in-flash.

Being introduced to the flash fiction genre was a pivotal moment for me as a writer. Like a lot of students, I started off with the first edition of *Sudden Fiction: American Short-Short Stories* edited by Robert Shapard and James Thomas. This book, which was assigned reading for a creative writing workshop, opened my eyes to new ways of telling stories. Not only did they appeal to my limited attention span, but they also appealed to my desire for immediacy, the possibility of getting in and out of something quickly. To be successful, every aspect of the story has to be on fire. What I think is so powerful about that book is that most of the writers were not necessarily writing in a form but rather were writing stories that worked naturally and happened to fit that genre. Reading "Popular Mechanics" by Raymond Carver, for instance, changed my idea of what a story can be. In the story, a recently separated couple fight over who gets to take their baby, each one pulling and grabbing until the harrowing line: "In this manner, the issue was decided." It is unsettling and unsatisfying but in a gratifying way. The story lets us in for an intense glimpse and ushers us out before we could ever get comfortable. Carver makes us not the spectator of a brutal crime, but the generator of one, because the reader is forced to contemplate what happens next. He tells us it has been decided but we are left to decide how. Each moment, from the bedroom to the kitchen, is so clearly realized that we do not expect to shift so suddenly to such vague language after he did so much of the work for us.

The story is jarringly effective and one that I look to when I feel I am overcomplicating a scene and need a way out. I imagine that Carver wrote himself into a corner and found a miraculous way to escape. It's a trick you can only do once, but imagining him getting there is an inspiration: I want each of my stories to end with some aspect lingering in the reader's head.

In our lives, we are sometimes only allowed glimpses into other people's lives, singular moments with characters we will never deeply know. How we twist and turn what we have seen or heard or felt into narratives has always been fascinating to me. I've always loved fragments because they give me permission to fill in the blanks, to imagine the rest, and I think the novella-in-flash was the next logical step, to take these tiny pieces, each with a stand-alone agenda and glue them into a larger story.

While it's not a perfect example, and not exactly a work of flash fiction or even a novella, I always look to *Jesus' Son* by Denis Johnson as an innovator in interconnecting stories, compiling fragments that tell a complete narrative but not a fluid one. You end up with a cohesive portrait of a group of characters but not a traditional one where one story follows another. Each story could exist without the others and they are only connected with threads. You are reintroduced to characters far removed from their previous settings and part of the fun is imagining all that happened in between. The final portrait is complete, but it's nevertheless in pieces, scattered around the floor, but still in the same room. Not all of your questions are answered, nor should they be.

With that goal in mind, one of the hardest parts about working in the novella-in-flash form is making decisions about what stories have direct impact and which ones are simply set-ups for stories to come or informational. A lot of the stories that were left out of *The Family Dogs* after editing were the bridge stories, the ones that made a lot of the other stories make a lot more "sense." While it seems like a lot to ask a reader, my expectation is that the readers of this genre are already ready and willing to undertake the challenge of building their own bridges. In the end, I believe that a flash novella allows for these glimpses, introduced in fragments, to add up to a complete narrative arc. This genre allows for the reader to interact with the text, interpreting each story and being able to make narrative leaps. In *The Family Dogs*, I attempted to create a character in Al that exists completely inside this world of fragments and anecdotes and through his vision, my hope is that we start to see the family as a whole, much like you would learn about my family if you only listened to me. I might be under the illusion of control, but even my embellishments and falsehoods will still reveal me and my family in the end.

When I was eight years old, I was responsible for the deaths of at least eight rabbits. It's either really interesting or really depressing to note that I can't remember anything about my childhood without there being a significant amount of gum. When my family tells me that story, there is no gum, no excessive repetition, just the plain fact that I was responsible for the rabbits dying. We nod our heads, I take it in, acknowledge that it was ridiculous and awful and sort of hilarious, especially if you don't know the whole story. We drive by that spot on the street and the story is stuck there, the rabbits are still under the wheels. In reality, when I was eight years old in that scene, I was crying uncontrollably and it was one of my earliest memories of feeling utterly helpless and alone, but there are few things more painful than imagining a desperate child sobbing over the corpses of recently adorable rabbits—those are the kind of details that ruin perfectly good stories. Sometime the true story takes too long and has too many moving parts and it wouldn't be worth retelling. My version is weaker than my family's version. I'm too focused on the gum and their focus is right where it should be, on the fact that I chased at least eight rabbits to their deaths, right over there. The tale has to be told fast because the spot where my brother buried the candy bars that he shoplifted from Walgreens is coming right up and that's a much better story.

—CHRIS BOWER

THE FAMILY DOGS

A NOVELLA-IN-FLASH IN TWO PARTS
BY CHRIS BOWER

TABLE OF CONTENTS

PART 1 | **A L**

MOM

IT WAS A CLOUDY DAY IN EARLY APRIL, and Mom was swimming in Lake Michigan. She was neck deep flapping her arms in pain, not because it was early April and snowing, and not because her body was numb and blue, and not because she had fallen off a boat or been discarded in either a cruel practical joke or an elaborate ransom drop-off.

No, Mom was out there screaming because she had just begun giving birth to me.

Dad and my brother Matt were watching her from the beach and, just like that Stephen Crane story, they waved back at her. Even our dog, Peggy, showed more concern. She ran onto the dark sand and barked at Mom before the tide rushed over her paws and sent her cowering back to the beach towels.

Inside, inside my mom, I heard those tiny barks, and I remember asking, "What are those beautiful sounds?"

Mom swam toward the beach, her arms making huge splashes.

Dad laughed and said, "Look at that, Matt. That's your mother for life. What do you think about that, smart guy?"

Matt looked down at his feet and imagined what would happen if they suddenly became giant crabs. He wondered if he would have enough control over them to claw my dad apart, or if they would simply scurry down a little hole and suck the rest of his body after them. Then he wondered if they even had crabs like that around here, and by the time he was done wondering and Dad was done laughing, my mother was already on the beach, lying on the cold sand panting, pushing me out.

During my birth Mom swore a lot, but not like in the movies. She swore a lot even when she wasn't giving birth. She used to swear at me when I did bad things and also when I did good things. When she said, "Oh that's fucking great," to me it could easily have gone either way, and at three it was a true test of my intellect to discern the subtle changes in her tone. I so often failed those tests that I was not able to have an honest conversation with her true voice until I was a teenager. When I turned thirteen she said to me, while she was sick at the hospital, "You're not a fucking baby anymore," and I understood exactly what she meant.

During my birth, Dad did not have a video camera. He didn't faint at the sight of blood or at the sound of his wife in horrific pain. No, he did not faint that day, but he did, as he lovingly continued to do for the rest of his life, drink beer out of cans until he passed out. Before they left the house for the beach, he had filled his big blue cooler with giant silver cans of beer. After he had finished loading them in, he said, "You could never get away with a cooler like this in July, not with all those shorts-wearing beach cops checking under cozies and sniffing water bottles, you won't. Going to the beach now, with this cooler, is like getting away with murder."

He told Mom he was going to lie down for a while and was snoring next to his cooler about five feet from her as Matt very carefully removed one big can of beer after another to use as load-bearing poles in his giant frozen sandcastle.

A few hours later when I finally fell out, I landed in a hole Matt had reluctantly dug for me on Mom's orders. I landed there in the amniotic fluid, blood, and water that had washed in from the lake. Peggy kept trying to drink out of the hole, but Matt kept pulling her away, her mouth dripping yellow and red liquid into the sand. Matt kept saying, "Bad dog, bad dog."

I remember thinking to myself and trying to ask, "What is that beautiful thing?" but all that came out was a little baby scream.

Mom picked my little red and blue body up and I was covered in sand from head to toe as she held me in her arms whispering sweetly, things like, "Hi there, you cute little shit."

"Wake up your fucking father, Matt," she said.

"I'm awake," Dad said, opening his eyes.

"Don't you want to see your goddamn son?" she asked.

"I can see. What do you want to call him?"

She cleaned some of the sand off my face and asked, squinting her eyes, "Who does he look like?"

Matt looked at me and said, "I think he looks like a sand monster."

Peggy barked at Matt like she was trying to say something and then chased a white cup that blew by my birth. And when I first opened my eyes, I saw her there, her mouth filled with a bloody Styrofoam paste.

Mom looked to Dad and said, "Shit. Aren't you going to say something?"

"Like what?"

"Like, maybe welcome him into the goddamn family?"

Dad looked at me, took my tiny hand in his and said, "Welcome to the goddamn family, sand monster."

WILEY

MATT BROKE HIS LEG SLIDING DOWN THE BANISTER. So we got rid of the banister.

I broke my arm flying off the stairs. So we got rid of the stairs.

We all slept together on the pull-out couch, and Dad ran the microwave as our alarm clock, so all night we heard that round glass tray circling in vain.

After a week everyone was bothering everyone else and Dad was on the phone hiring back the guys who took our stairs and our banister, but before they could come, Matt realized that nobody had been feeding Wiley, his fish. He stood where the stairs had been and yelled up to Wiley, telling him where his food was and advising him on how to hop out and hop back in his tank; telling him how long it was safe to be out of the water and asking if he wouldn't mind closing the window so the rain didn't get on his baseball cards.

For a while I thought Matt had really lost it, because he wouldn't stop laughing and crying at the same time. Mom finally calmed him down by telling him that Wiley was fine, "Because the ghosts are feeding Wiley. Because that's what ghosts are for."

We all very much liked this explanation.

IRELAND

THE SUMMER I WAS ELEVEN, my parents sent me to Ireland to live with my aunt. But since my parents are on both sides German, I didn't have an aunt in Ireland.

I had a good time anyway, sleeping in green glens, admiring stone fences, riding roaming cows from town to town, going to church a lot, and polishing up on my whistling.

When the summer was over my brogue was thick and lovely, and after I told my parents what had happened and where I had been, my dad said it had been a good learning experience for all of us.

INVENTIONS

DAD INVENTED A BASEBALL BAT that could swing itself. There was a hinge near the bottom of the bat that was voice-activated, and as the ball approached all you had to do was yell, "Swing," and it swung.

Despite the genius of it all, it wasn't really any fun. But when we humored him, he knew it, so he stashed it away inside his "mistake box" filled with other mistakes like the fake bush you could fit over real fire hydrants that was partially responsible, along with me, a lighter, and a gas-soaked effigy of a girl I liked but who didn't like me, for burning our first house triumphantly to the ground.

PEGGY

SHE NEVER RAN AWAY ON PURPOSE but she always ran away. She would follow her stomach, smelling the garbage cans in the alley, moving can to can until she was blocks from home. We'd find her by following the fallen receptacles and they would eventually lead us to Peggy, on some old lady's porch, eating out of a house dish with her eyes down, focused on something hearty and delicious the old lady had probably prepared for herself.

Mom said that old ladies always made more food than they needed because they missed their husbands and children and were always expecting company.

When Peggy finished her meal—and she'd always finish her meal—she'd look at us with recognition and walk slowly down the steps. She'd nod her head at the old ladies, quietly saying thank you. Mom would offer them money, but the old ladies would always refuse and we'd always have the feeling that the women wanted to say, but didn't say, "She's welcome back anytime."

Peggy would walk right past us and lead the way home.

It was never the same porch and never the same old lady.

Dad once said to Mom after hearing one of these stories, "Sometimes old ladies have husbands."

Mom said, "Yes," pushing a kitchen drawer closed. "But they'd prefer not to, and to miss them instead."

GRANDMA

She used to help draw people's blood over at the Catholic Hospital. She came over to our house one day after work, her white blouse splattered red, and from her I learned that even volunteers can be fired.

MATT

MATT SLEEPWALKED to the twenty-four-hour pet store and bought himself a pony. He sleep-walked home and woke us all up with the noisy little leash that came with and amplified the presence of his pony.

My parents woke him up and made him walk it back. Matt was embarrassed because he had always hated ponies.

A few hours later he came home with three thousand dollars, and he didn't know what he wanted to spend it on because he had never had that much before. The only thing he said he didn't want was another pony.

When Matt came to my pillow at night, he told me how magical that walk back had been. That little mutated horse, he said, made him feel alive.

"I'll never feel that alive again," he said.

"Maybe you should get a pony," I said. "Buy one when you're awake with all that money."

And before Matt punched me to sleep, he told me that he was sorry.

HEAD

WHEN I WAS SIX, MY HEAD HAD A TOASTER IN IT. Dad said it was broken, because it only cooked on one side. I told him to just flip the bread over in the middle. His palm hit my temple and he asked me how it got broken.

SAUSAGES

PEGGY ONCE CLIMBED AN APPLE TREE and had to be coaxed down with sausages.

Matt didn't believe me so I brought him, Peggy, and some sausages to the tree in the park where it happened.

"So this is where it happened," I said, pointing to a long thick branch. "I turned around and there she was, right up there. I couldn't get her down and had to run home to get sausages. When I got back, she was sleeping up there."

Matt said, "Dogs don't climb trees, Al, it's just not something they can do."

I said to him sternly, "It happened and it will happen again. Why do you think we call her Peggy?"

"What does that even mean, Al?" said Matt.

We both looked at Peggy and Peggy sat in the grass, salivating at the sausages in my hand. After ten minutes of waiting I said, "She is only not doing it because she already knows about the sausages. We'll have to come back tomorrow."

Matt put his arm around me and asked, "Are you sure you didn't dream it?"

"Of course not," I said, shaking his arm off.

I fed Peggy her reward, knowing that it was his fault that

Peggy was not in the tree. She didn't trust him. Not the way she trusted me; but I didn't have the heart to tell him.

BABY

I ONCE SAW A BABY WRESTLE AN ALLIGATOR in Florida. Mom covered my eyes and screamed, "This isn't fucking fair."

The guy who owned the alligator said, "Wait until he swallows him and throws up."

The guy who owned the baby said, "Charlie's more of a sucker than a swallower."

I think they both misheard my mom.

TEN

WHEN I WAS TEN, I HAD A KITE and I put it under a rock and ran around with the string, flapping my wings. Matt and his friend Fat Sammy laughed at me for a while, but stopped when I flew over them and crapped on their new haircuts.

.

GRANDPA

EVERY SUNDAY WE WOULD GO over to my grandparents' and go to the 10 o'clock Mass. Grandpa was always sitting there in the living room in his chair drinking martinis and eating nuts. When we would walk from their house to church I always asked, "Why doesn't Grandpa go to church?" and they always said the same thing: "Grandpa goes to the 12 o'clock Mass."

One Sunday afternoon I was riding my bike with my parents after church and we were going to stop for ice cream, but my mom saw Grandpa's mangled old green bike leaning into a broken window. Workers were sweeping up glass from the street and sitting inside the shop on a stool was Grandpa, with a clump of paper towels sopping up the blood on his face.

I looked at my Swatch watch and it was 12:15. "Let's go some place else," Mom said quickly and we rode away.

The next Sunday, my grandfather was sitting in his chair eating olives off the spears in his glass. He had a Band-Aid on his liver spotted forehead.

On the way to church I asked, "Why was Grandpa at the ice cream parlor when he should have been at church?"

"He was on his way to church," they told me. "And he rode

his bike through the window because he was confused." They told me he got up and ordered three scoops of peanut butter and chocolate in a cup and no spoon. He had his own in his pocket wrapped up in a napkin.

When I asked Grandma recently about this story, she told it exactly the same way except when she got to the spoon my grandmother said, "That was his downfall. Don't carry around silverware."

"Was Grandpa an alcoholic, Grandma?" I asked, and she said, staring off into a window sealed shut with layers of bad paint jobs, "Of course he was."

BELLA

I HAD A COUSIN NAMED BELLA about my age who lived in Maine. He came to visit one summer and had a really slow stupid accent that was a big hit with the slow stupid girls on my block.

One day when we were playing basketball in my alley, Bella fell and knocked over the sunflower Matt was growing in the garden. Matt wasn't mad. Matt said he was happy that day to see his sunflower fall. It made him learn something about himself.

"Tough guys don't cry over dead flowers," he said as he kicked it into the garden. I told him someone should put that line on a t-shirt, but he didn't, and I didn't, and as far as I know nobody else did.

But I'll never forget sneaking out that night with Bella and Matt and hearing my father cry at the sight of Matt's fallen sunflower. With tears in our eyes, we dug its long and skinny but wide and round on top grave.

JEWELRY

WHEN I WAS SMALL MOM USED TO HOLD ME in her palm, cupping me with her fingers. She didn't have unusually large hands, I was just unusually small.

Dad used to say, "Don't hold him like that. He's not a piece of jewelry."

"Yes he is," Mom said.

"Can you wear him out to dinner?" he asked.

Mom replied, "Will you take me out to dinner?"

And Dad said, "Fine, he's a piece of jewelry."

DEATH

WHEN I WAS TEN AND BEGAN TO WORRY about death, I started to save everything that was important to me, even if it meant destroying it. I dismantled my bicycle and hid the pieces in my closet, put the banana seat in a shoe box and the handlebars in a paper grocery bag. I also took all of the remotes for the television and VCR, which I had become fond of and was afraid to lose. I hid them inside a used paper lunch bag. On the bag, Mom had written:

> *Al,*
> *Tuna Fish, Carrots, Apple Juice.*
> *Don't lose your gloves.*

Dad searched for weeks for the remotes. He tore the TV room apart, pulling the bed out of the couch over and over again, patting down the wrinkled sheets. He even considered looking inside the dog. Instead of getting new remotes, he just decided which channel he was going to watch the whole day so he didn't have to get up.

At night in bed, I'd get the remotes down and point them out the window at cars and trees and people walking by and pretend to change the world.

I saved Peggy by cutting off pieces of her hair, filling plastic sandwich bags until they could barely be sealed. I hid them inside my pillow until there was no need for the pillow.

HANDS

WHEN MOM'S RIGHT HAND was in the hospital, a dog's head lived where her hand had been. It was a good, not great dog, quiet and pretty, not like me.

He used to sneak under the table at dinner looking for food. Mom would be eating the dinner she made with her left hand and I'd be feeding the dog parts of the dinner that I didn't like. We all made each other happy.

Peggy didn't like him. She was jealous that he could sleep with my parents while she was stuck sleeping in the basement on the cement floor.

When Mom's hand came back, the dog disappeared. I asked her what happened to the dog.

"We didn't have time to even name him," I said. "That's the first thing you're supposed to do with a dog and we didn't do it. That's why he left. Another family is going to name him."

Mom said, with tenderness, as she rubbed my head with her two hands, "The dog's fucking dead, Al."

KIDS

IN THE SUMMER, when all the kids in the neighborhood were out playing games with complicated rules and simple brutality, or enterprising with overpriced beverage stands with stolen ingredients and dirty water, I'd start out playing with them.

I stood in the back as jobs were assigned and slowly backed up until I was hidden behind a tree. I'd then sneak through the bushes and go back home. I couldn't go through the front or back doors because I'd have to answer too many questions, so I snuck in through the basement window.

Peggy was down there waiting for me. I pushed open the paint-splattered window and she'd let me rest my feet on her back and help me down.

Dad yelled to Peggy from the top of the stairs. He said things like, "Come up now if you wanna take a shit." I held my breath. Sometimes she'd leave me and I'd take her place. Usually she'd come right back alone. Nobody ever came down to the basement.

On perfect summer days, Dad threw dog treats down the stairs and I put my head on her stomach and fell asleep listening to her eat and breathe.

DAD

DAD DOESN'T TALK MUCH when he's upset. He just throws things and waits for the perfect words to come to him to end the experience, almost like a chapter ending telling us to now move on to the next story.

When Mom died, Dad tossed the living room into the kitchen and the kitchen into the backyard. Matt and I were in the laundry room waiting to see where we'd be tossed.

Matt said, "Closet."

I said, "Basement."

Dad came in before we could go anywhere. His face was sweaty. His eyes were red and bulging. His hands were cut up and bleeding. He looked at us pushed up in the corner and asked, "Where's the goddamn dog?"

PART 2 | **MATT**

ORIGINS

WHEN I WAS A LITTLE BOY, Dad told me he found me while sailing. I was just a baby, clutching a buoy in the middle of Lake Michigan. He said the lower part of my body was covered with green junk. Mom had to scrape it off with sticks and pull old fish hooks out of my legs. He said that I was a good baby, that I didn't cry.

I used to cry when he told me that story.

Now, I prefer his version, believe his version, just for the hell of it. I believe it even though I know the closest Dad ever got to being in a boat was when he drove the Corolla under a bridge during a flash flood. He said we were going to be fine as the wheels hit the water, and he kept saying that as the car started to float. Mom said, "Now look what you fucking did!" And Dad said, "We're fine, we're going to be fine."

Al and I were in the backseat loving it, floating above the road. Peggy was in the backseat with us, barking at the water, and Dad kept yelling back at her, telling her to shut up, and Mom kept yelling at Dad asking him why he just turned our stupid little car into a stupid little boat as Dad turned the wheels in the water.

I don't remember how that story ends.

Dad told Al he found him in a swamp, floating on a little boat made out of sticks and hair, red hair that must have belonged to his real mother.

That's the point in the story where Mom always stepped in and said, "I'm your mother, Al. No matter what this man says."

Al liked this story.

He'd eat it up and smile like he was remembering it, seeing it in his head. When it ended, usually with Dad pulling him out of an alligator's mouth, Al would get frustrated and hurl a barrage of technical questions at Dad: "So how big was this boat? Was there a sail? Was I sleeping when you found me? Was I crying? Could you hear me in the water? How did you pull me in? With a fishing pole, with a paddle? What were you doing in a swamp?"

Dad always changed the details, which always bothered Al, and when Dad stopped telling it, Al started telling his own origin story, the way he wanted it to be. He got rid of the swamp, the boat, the hair, and the alligator. I haven't heard him tell a new one recently, but I think he basically just adapted mine and turned up the dramatics.

Mom and Dad didn't take pictures of us, not even as babies. It wasn't until we were older that we knew it wasn't normal, that usually families take too many pictures. Fathers have camcorders built into their palms, mothers ask complete strangers in front of monuments to take their picture, closets are filled with albums of photos of vacations, birthdays, graduations, Christmases. These are the things that people sometimes die for. Trying to save them in fires.

Do you know there isn't one picture of me opening a fucking Christmas present, riding a bike, playing with my dog, sitting on the goddamn toilet?

There is not even one picture of Al and me or the whole family together. All we have are individual, mandatory pictures—driver's licenses, school pictures—and those are just mug shots, pictures where you don't look like yourself because you aren't being yourself. You're just presenting evidence of your existence for people who want to match your face with a name, and believe me they're more dishonest than a posed family photo, everyone smiling on the stairs, holding onto the banister, everyone organized by height and age, because at least with a family photo you can imagine what happened before, what happened after, you can see the shit around the house, evidence of where you lived, clothes that you had in your closet. But a head shot at the DMV? The blank backdrop at the passport photo place? That's just evidence that you, at some point in time, had a fucking head.

When we asked Dad why he never took our picture, he said, "Film was too expensive."

When we asked Mom, she said, "Film was just too fucking expensive."

Those were both very unsatisfying answers.

I used to worry about this all the time, feeling I got cheated, and believe me, I'm still pissed, but I've come to terms with it because I know I can't go back and change anything now.

Al on the other hand, thinks he can.

After Mom died, he took it really hard that there was no documentation of his childhood, no pictures of him doing anything but fake smiling for school photos. He became obsessed and tried to collect all of the photos that may have been taken of him by other people's parents. He managed to get a few, but none that he liked because he was never the focus. He was always a kid in a crowd.

He tried to get me to help him re-create some of the things he wished were photographed. I told him I didn't care enough anymore, and that I didn't quite understand what he meant, that I didn't want to understand what he meant.

He said to me, "If you don't want to be in my childhood, you don't have to be, Matt. I'll write you out. I'll write everybody out. It will just be me."

ABOUT THE AUTHOR

CHRIS BOWER is a writer and teacher based in Chicago. He is the curator and host of the Ray's Tap Reading Series and a founding member of Found Objects Theatre Group. *Little Boy Needs Ride*, his book of short stories with illustrations by Susie Kirkwood, is forthcoming in 2015 from Curbside Splendor Publishing. You can find him at holdmyhorses.com.

ACKNOWLEDGMENTS

BETTY SUPERMAN By Tiff Holland

Thank you to the following journals for first publishing these stories:

"Dragon Lady" *Literary Potpourri*
"Hot Work" *Frigg*
"Betty Superman" *Denver Syntax*
"First Husband" *Smokelong Quarterly*
"The Barberton Mafia" *Prime Number II*
"Homing" *Frigg*

HERE, WHERE WE LIVE By Meg Pokrass

Grateful acknowledgment to the following journals, in which these pieces first appeared in different forms:

"Double Date" *Night Train*
"Fields of Cheese" *Unmovable Feast*
"Helium" *Camroc Press Review*
"Illusions" *Prick of the Spindle*

SHAMPOO HORNS By Aaron Teel

Thank you to the following journals for first publishing these stories:

"Broken English" *Tin House*
"The Widow's Trailer" *Brevity*
"Tater's Nipple" *North Texas Review*

BELL AND BARGAIN By Margaret Patton Chapman

Thanks so much to Abigail Beckel and Kathleen Rooney at Rose Metal Press; thanks to Kelcey Parker for her advice, to Kyle Beachy and Chris Bower for their thoughtful reading, and to Chris again for thinking I had a novella in the first place; thanks to those who read and supported this work in its earlier forms, including Dan Beachy-Quick, Sarah Levine, Beth Nugent, Janet Desaulniers, Liz Birch, Tom D'Angelo, and David Metcalf; and to the Catwalk Institute, the Vermont Studio Center, and the City of Chicago Cultural Center.

Thanks also to Max Wilson and Lynette Acosta for telling me the story about the little girl who was born speaking, and to my other friends and family whose stories I have stolen and put in here.

And thank you, Tony, most of all.

THE FAMILY DOGS By Chris Bower

The story "Mom" was previously published as "The Family Dog" in 2008 in *Proximity: Education as Art*, Issue 1.

A play written and directed by Chris Bower with the name *The Family Dogs*, containing similar plot elements and dialogue, was performed at the Rhinoceros Theater Festival in 2007.

I would like to thank Wayne and Roberta Bower for being wonderful and supportive parents and for surrounding me with such interesting characters. I would also like to thank Beau O'Reilly, Scott Barsotti, Matt Wilson, and F. Tyler Burnett for bringing these characters to life on stage so I could properly put them back on the page.

A NOTE ABOUT THE TYPE

The text of this book is set in Crimson, an open source typeface inspired by Oldstyle faces and their designers. As a libre type project, Crimson is ever-evolving, pulling from such classic faces as Hoefler Text, Baskerville, and Minion for inspiration, and reinventing itself for both print and digital design. Sebastian Kosch, a previously inexperienced designer, began work on Crimson in April 2010, and continues to release updates. As an amalgam of traditional faces, Crimson appears slightly rounder and more stable on the page as a result of less contrast between strokes, unlike the garaldes it is modeled after. Curves and bells are gentler and more organic than the calligraphic strokes present in other book faces.

Bebas Neue, the display face, was designed by Ryoichi Tsunekawa for the Dharma Type project. Similar in appearance to more common favorites like Alternate Gothic and Din, Bebas Neue makes crisp turns in evenly weighted strokes. Flattened curves along the baseline and an overall geometric appearance makes Bebas Neue command the page with minimal text.

Used in combination in the text and on the cover, Bebas Neue and Crimson encompass the newness and excitement of the novella-in-flash form, with modern lines and sensibilities, bold statements, and subtle nuances. Yet behind the unique and malleable form is a simple dedication—a continuation of tradition—to putting words to page.

—EMILY KENT